HOT ENOUGH TO MELT CHOCOLATE

Quinn Family Series

Novella One

LARO CLAITTY

LADERO FICTION published by

Ladero Press LLC

229 Kettering Road

Deltona, Florida 32725

First Ladero Press Printing, March 2017

Printed in the United States of America

Set in Palatino Linotype

Cover Designed by Jeanette Harrell

www.laderopress.com

www.laroclaitty.com

Printed in U.S.A.

In Memory of Adel (née Lopez) Norris

*You loaned me your Harlequin when we were young ladies,
and I have been on a romance journey ever since.
From Australia to Jamaica to Vancouver, I have travelled the
world through romance novels. It has been a thrill to go to some of
the places between those pages and realize
they were indeed as written.*

*Thank you very much for trading books! (I almost feel sorry for
how quickly I put down those SWEET VALLEY HIGH books.
Almost.)*

*I am so happy to know that you experienced a Harlequin story
of your very own.*

*May you enjoy the grandest of romances as you rest in God's
eternal love in the grandest of locales.*

*Adelaida Marciala Norris
1972-2017*

Acknowledgements

Truly, when one writes a book, one gets an understanding of the concept of "it takes a village". This book has certainly required different people in different roles. I am thankful to God for His faithfulness and giving me all I needed to complete this journey.

For riding around San Diego and talking about dating—a conversation that led to this storyline so many years ago—thank you, my cousin, Latoya Long. May you experience a grand romance—one that makes a book pale in comparison.

To the prereaders who provided such helpful feedback, thank you: (Auntie) Stephanie Jenkins, (Sister of My Heart) Demetrica Tyson, (Auntie) Barbara Thompson, (Auntie) Betty Eudell, (Cousin) Scharika Richardson, and (Auntie) Barbara Robinson.

For unknowingly inspiring me to finish this book, thank you, Ms. Dorothy Mayhue. (And, I got Jeanette on the team!)

For hosting the Community Business Showcase Workshop and getting on the phone to make contacts on the spot, thank you so much, Angie Bee. My cousin is a wise man to have gotten you to join #TeamBartee.

To my friends, thank you for giving your honest feedback, clicking "Like", and all the many ways you support the vision and support me. I love you much.

Mims Rouse, thank you, Friend. #IHaveAQuestionForYou

To my family, you have always been a reason for me to keep stretching, keep reaching, and keep trying. Thank you for being an ever-present cheer team. It is not every day that a woman gets such large families with such gracious love that is readily shared. It is my prayer that I continue to demonstrate your unending love for me. Love you much!

To my text/read this/tell me what you think team—whether it's day or night or *really* late night—I surely do love you much. Dad, Mom, Tiff, Leroy, Jerry, Jan, and Jamie, thank you so very much.

For every one still believing that *the* grand romance can be yours: may you never be too shocked by love's packaging to open it and give it a try.

ENOUGH TO MELT
CHOCOLATE

Chapter 1

"Hmm. Right there. Back a bit. Yeah. That hits the spot."

Antoinette Quinn, or Toni as her family and friends called her, kept her head thrown back, luxuriating in the absolute decadence of such treatment. She understood why people would miss work or make deals for just a couple hours of pleasure. *Few things in life compare to this kind of pleasure,* she thought to herself, *Men and women alike sacrifice for just this.* Raising her head from the pleasure bowl, Toni looked around the chic salon and saw others in the shampoo area looking at her strangely.

"What?" she breathily asked of the spectators.

"What do you mean "what?" asked Tara, her purveyor of pleasure. "They're looking at you because you are over here acting like this is midnight on Cinemax. You are the only client we have who is so vocal about getting her hair shampooed."

"But they are soooo good. I thoroughly enjoy having my hair washed. All that massaging—smooth at times and a bit rough at others. It works, though. *Every* single time."

Tara led her from the shampoo area into the prepping area to give her a roller set. Toni had long hair that was worn in its naturally curly state most of the time, but occasionally, she enjoyed the break from styling her hair— took far too much time in the mornings. So, this salon visit, she was having her hair curled. As president and consultant for her own business, she needed all the extra minutes in her day that she could get.

After a number of minutes under the dryer, Toni was led to the lounge area where she could relax with some tea and her book until her stylist was ready. She sat down in the lounge with other women who were also waiting to be styled or anticipating other treatments. Tuning out the conversation, she proceeded to read the latest novel from one of the top African-American romance writers. Eventually, the low volume conversation caught her attention.

"I wouldn't date a man from a different culture. I am strictly chocolate," stated one woman with a wrap that was presumably going to be curled or flat-ironed.

"Why not? Men are men," stated the sister with graying locs that were about to be re-twisted.

Toni tried to continue with her book, but it was impossible. She and her girlfriends had just had this conversation in which she had stated the same thing as the first woman. Toni definitely preferred African-American men.

"Would you date a man from a different culture?" asked one of the women of Toni.

"Who me?" Toni queried, looking up from her book.

"Yes, you. Would you date a man from a different culture?"

"Hmm. Absolutely not. No, I'm with the woman over there. I am strictly chocolate," she replied.

"Even if he were hot?" the woman kept on with her questioning.

"Hot? He'd have to be *very* hot to melt *this* chocolate," Toni threw out, causing the other women to break into giggles.

"Well, now," the woman with the graying locs exclaimed, "that is some kind of hot!"

Toni left the salon intent on getting her errands done for the day. While she was out and about, she figured she should call her parents, since she lived in sunny San Diego and they lived on the opposite coast in sunny Florida. She pulled out her cell phone as she sashayed her way down the street, looking fabulous with her newly coiffed hair and with somebody's name stamped on her chest. Occasionally, Toni liked to look young and hip, although thirty-six was staring her in the face. Hence, a famous designer stamped across her chest. *All that free advertisement*, she often thought to herself.

"Hey, Ma. It's me, Toni," she told her mother after she answered.

"Hey, Baby. I know it's you, Antoinette. I gave birth to you, you know," replied her mother, Regina, with her usual greeting.

It was a running joke between Toni and her sister, Sherise, and her brother, Alex, about their mother's greeting. They often burst into laughter when recalling how their mother answered all of them in the same manner.

"Ma, I know you know who I am, but I just have to say it. Didn't we just have this conversation two days ago?" she teasingly asked her mother.

"Yes, so I don't know why after almost thirty-six years you won't stop," her mother teased in return. Her mom had a great sense of humor and kept her family in stitches.

"Well, how are you today? How's Daddy?"

"We're fine. Your daddy claims he's going to clean out the garage today. He needs more space for his new car, you know. A sixty-five-year-old man with a Porsche? Go figure. Darryl's worked hard, so he may as well enjoy it. Anyway, he's fine, and so am I. How're things with you?"

"Fine—," Toni started to reply, while heading to the nearest boutique coffee shop for her four-dollar cup of milk and sugar.

"You know I talked to Reecie, that sister of yours. That girl is working too hard trying to make partner. I told her that Rome was not built in a day. Talk to her, please. Anyway, how are you, baby?"

"Fine, Ma. Work is good, and the company is doing well. Although, since the company is just me, it should be doing wonderful, shouldn't it? Anyway, I'm wrapping up a contract; I have a meeting with a potential client on Tuesday. Hopefully, it goes well. Although I could use a break, I gotta "work while it's day", as you say."

"You'll be fine. Just don't get like Reecie. She's younger than you by two years, but working like she's about to take over the White House. Tell her to slow down, please."

"I will."

"Anyway. Let me go so that I can get dinner ready. Your daddy went fishing, and we're having fresh fish. Thankfully, he's good about cleaning and filleting the fish. Makes cooking it a pleasure. I love you, baby. Be good."

"I love you, too, Mama. Give Daddy a hug and kiss for me. Bye."

Reaching the coffee shop, Toni took her place in line after dropping her phone in her handbag. *Why are there so many people willing to plunk down good money for coffee— in a paper cup, no less? Including me?*

As she waited, the person in front of her began to catch her attention. She began to notice things about him. Nice hair. *Well, he takes care of his hair, for sure.* Her eyes moved lower. Nice broad shoulders. *Hmm, quite nice, if I say so myself.* Her eyes moved even lower. *This ain't a black man, but that sure is a black man's butt*, she smirked to herself, running her tongue across her bottom lip.

Suddenly, the man turned around and asked, "Would you care to see my front, too?"

Mortified, Toni looked up into one of the most handsome faces she had ever seen. "Excuse me?" she asked.

"My front," he said again, pointing a lean and stronglooking white finger towards the mirror behind the counter that showed all activity in the coffee shop. "I saw you doing a survey of my back. Did I pass?"

"I'm sorry. I didn't mean to be rude. You, umm, have lovely hair," Toni stuttered.

"Really? My hair, huh?" he replied with his eyebrow raised over distinct, dark green eyes in disbelief at her "lovely hair" comment. "Thank you."

"Next," called out the barista from behind the counter.

"Umm, it's your turn. She's calling you."

"Hmm. You didn't answer my question. Did I pass your inspection?" he repeated.

"Umm. Yes. Please. Turn around. She is giving me the eye. You know how they can get if you don't place your order quick enough."

The very fine, very handsome white man turned around and placed his order, but not before giving her a wink from those gorgeous eyes and turning up those full lips in a flirtatious smirk. Toni let out a huge inward sigh after he left without even looking at her. *That's what I get for inspecting him like he's meat. Lord, he's hot enough to melt chocolate. He gives whole new meaning to "eye candy".* Toni chuckled at realizing that she had spouted those words with such bravado not too long ago in the salon. *Well, at least I won't have to test my theory.* She placed her order, left the shop, and went about the rest of the day.

Toni's "eye candy" left the coffee shop and drove home after getting his coffee. The short, but highly interesting conversation with the very attractive woman offered a lot more stimulation than his cup of caffeine. Clear, chocolate skin covered a tall and nicely shaped body that captured his attention as soon as she stepped into line after him. She was not skinny as so many women these days seemed to think was attractive. *I could get used to that*, he thought. Of course, he could not accost the woman in the shop, but he'd had a good time watching *her* check *him* out in the coffee shop's mirror. The look on her face after he'd called her game was priceless. She actually blushed from embarrassment. If she came his way again—a long shot in the widespread metropolitan area of San Diego—he'd go with his gut and ask her out. After all, all she could say was "no" and that, in his opinion, would be a shame.

Chapter 2

Accomplishing all she planned to for the day, Toni arrived at her home on the northwest side of San Diego. A number of clients for her process improvement and appraisal business were along the I-5/I-805 business corridor. To make it easier to get to clients, she lived sandwiched between the communities of Clairemont and La Jolla. While traffic was quite considerable, it was not as bad as that of some other metropolitan areas. Toni still thought it wise to be strategically located to serve clients. Getting to downtown was easy enough by heading south on either highway. Coming from Florida where water was abundant, the proximity to the beaches from her current residence was a great advantage, too.

After opening the front door, Toni walked across the hardwood cherry floor towards the kitchen which was located in the center of the house. Dropping her handbag and packages onto the counter, she washed her hands at the kitchen sink and went to the refrigerator. She was famished. While surveying the contents of the 'fridge, her mind went back to today's coffee shop scene as had been the case all day.

She could not get that man out of her mind despite all attempts to do so. *Gorgeous!* She was still mortified and shocked to have been caught checking him out! She thought what her sister Reecie would say. Toni was clearly the big sister, but Reecie had a lot more dating experience than Toni. How she managed to have a lively social life while working to "take over the White House" as their mother stated, Toni did not have a clue. She was so busy with her business and making sure clients were happy, dating was last on Toni's list of things to do. Reecie, however, managed to go out several times a week—sometimes with different guys in the same week—in man-strapped Washington, D.C., at that. *Heck, she should be voted into the White House on that accomplishment alone*, Toni laughingly thought to herself. She'd worked for a couple of years in metro D.C. and could testify to the black male landscape—male landscape period. Some days, it left a whole lot to be desired for the serious, mature woman seeking a grown-up relationship without the games and drama. Even "successful" men could not seem to leave the drama behind.

Pulling shrimp from the freezer, along with whipping cream, parmesan cheese, and butter from the refrigerator, Toni decided on shrimp alfredo. She was a good cook. She and her siblings had learned from their mother Regina, so she often cooked at home. She enjoyed eating out as well as the next person, but she enjoyed her kitchen with its many gadgets and appliances more. She knew how to use them, too, and thought it a waste if she didn't. While she prepared to cook, she stopped to flip the switch on the undercounter stereo system for some music. What came on in the shuffle was Jill Scott's "Lyzel in E Flat". Yes, Mr. Gorgeous White Man was causing her to contemplate all *kinds* of things. Toni laughed out loud as she continued to prepare her dinner. Since there was nothing she could do about *him*, she turned her thoughts to her upcoming client meeting on Tuesday.

If she received this contract, she would have a chance to stay close to home for a while. She often traveled to other parts of the country if she didn't have clients in San Diego.

Lately, though, work had been plentiful nearby, easing the need for travel. She had been on the road, working in various parts of the country for a number of years. Having a home base was a pleasant change of pace.

She was meeting with the company's president and vice presidents for Information Technology and Human Resources. The company was locally headquartered but had two other offices in Chicago and oddly enough, Orlando, Florida. The oddity was not about Orlando itself, but that she had not heard of the company and she was from central Florida. She would have to do some more research over the weekend. Grabbing one of the ever-present notepads scattered around the house, Toni made a note to find out a bit more about her potential client. She was finishing up her meal when her telephone rang. She looked at the caller ID and saw that it was none other than Reecie. Toni had her own nickname for her in the form of "Reece", as well.

"Hey, Reecie. What's up?"

"I'm just getting in from a most boring date. Since it's still early on your side of the country and I cut the date short, I thought I'd give you a call."

"Good. You know your mother Regina wanted me to call you anyway. As if we don't talk every couple of days. Nevertheless, you're helping me keep my word. Your mother is concerned about how hard you're working. She told me that you are working like you are, and I quote, "about to take over the White House," Toni dutifully reported to her sister. "She wants you to slow down. Translated, she wants you to come home for a visit so that she can see that you haven't been devoured by the bad boys of D.C."

"Why is she always *my* mother when you're calling to pass along a message?" Sherise teasingly replied. "She shouldn't worry. I'm going home for a visit this weekend. I didn't tell her because she needs to not know something one of these days. Daddy knows, but she doesn't. You know how she is—concerned about her "babies" as if we aren't grown. Speaking of which, have you heard from baby brother Alex?"

"Yes, he called me last night while he was in Chicago. They won last night so he was on a bit of a high considering it is nearing playoff time. He's ready for a break, though. Traveling so much is tiring. I reminded him that this is the life he wanted, so take it as it is, and enjoy it while it lasts."

"Our baby brother is a professional ball player. Even after all this time, it is still hard to believe. Anyway, he's been talking about retiring in a few more years. He's thirty-one now and says he's ready to get married and doesn't want to spend months on the road while married. I told him that was a wise decision considering all the things we've heard in the news about other traveling ball players."

"Yes, he mentioned that, so I guess he's thinking about it seriously."

"Umm hmm. So, how's your love life, Big Sister?" Reecie asked.

"Nonexistent. Next."

"That was too quick. Normally, you give me some spiel about how hard you're working and such. So, what gives? Did you meet someone?"

"No, I did not meet someone. It's "nonexistent" as I said."

"Hmm. You haven't met *anyone*? Have you at least *seen* a man that was appealing to you?"

"Well…I did see a guy in the coffee shop today. He was gorgeous. Tall and nicely fit. He was also white."

"Well, I bet that threw Miss "Strictly Chocolate" for a loop," Reecie jokingly replied.

"It's not like I will see him again, but, Reece, the man was yummy. Hot! Dark curly hair, dark green eyes, one fine behind, and a beautiful smile to go with all that," Toni replied on a wistful sigh.

"How did you get to see his smile and catalogue all that?"

"I got caught checking him out, if you must know."

Reecie hooted—loud—through the phone lines. "You finally got caught, huh? I told you that one day you would! Checking out men and cataloguing them like a record in one of your databases. "White male, 6'3", dark curly hair, dark green eyes, straight teeth." So, how did you get caught?"

"He saw me checking him out in the mirror behind the counter as I stood behind him in line. I was so embarrassed. Almost thirty-six and I get caught scoping out a man. Ridiculous. He had a nice butt, though. Like a brother's."

"Didn't your mother tell you that the butts will get you every time?" Reecie laughed down the line again.

"Yes, which is why I don't think I'm going to see this butt again. A shame since it was hot enough to melt chocolate, girl!" Toni told Reecie about the conversation the ladies had in the salon.

"You remember, don't you, that you don't date white men?"

"Yes. I leave that to you. You do a fine job of covering all the groups. How you get time to be a hot shot family attorney is beyond me, but somehow you manage."

"Priorities, baby. All about priorities. I want to get married soon, so I need to know who and what is out there before making a decision. Work is first, mind you. But surveying candidates is next. I'm an EOD—an Equal Opportunity Dater."

"So, that's what the young'uns call it these days, huh? Surveying? An EOD? Girl, you need to quit!"

"Yes, surveying. I don't sleep with all these men, so I'm okay. You know Alex would freak out if he thought I did—much less your mother and father."

"Well, continue to be safe on your surveying missions. I'm going to go. I need to get some paperwork done in order to submit the final bill to this last client. I love you, sweetie."

"Love you, too, Big Sis. Have a good night."

"Do the same."

Toni dropped the phone back on its base, put away her dinner dishes, and headed to her office. She worked a while to complete the paperwork on the last client. She wanted to ensure she invoiced them in a timely manner so that she could be paid in the same way. They were good about it, but sometimes clients wanted to drag their feet on payment.

After finishing, she decided to go to her potential client's web site and do a bit of research. She looked at the executives' names and saw that she would be meeting with Samuel Lawson, Gabriel Jackson, and Jessica Adams. Respectively, they held the positions of president, vice president of Information Technology, and vice president of Human Resources. She signed off after taking notes—the public web site did not have pictures, except for the president—and decided that Tuesday should be an interesting day.

Chapter 3

Tuesday dawned in true San Diego spring fashion—bright blue and not a cloud in the sky. Although she had been in Southern California—*SoCal* to the natives—for a little over two years, she still wasn't used to the constant blue skies. Before coming out West on a contract, Toni had worked in the cold Northeastern part of the country where sometimes deep into spring, it was necessary to wear an overcoat to combat the cold temperatures. She did not miss the cold or the gray, snow-laden skies.

Looking in her closet after tearing her eyes away from the gorgeous scenery beyond her window and getting up out of her cozy bed, Toni perused the contents of her closet to see what she would wear today. The world of information technology was decidedly less dressy than other industries, but because this was an initial presentation to a potential client, she needed to dress up. After much thought—her packed but neat closet gave her plenty to ponder when getting dressed—Toni decided upon a black Donna Karan pant suit with a tailored heavy silk cream shell she'd purchased from Talbots. It nipped in the waist and hugged her generous breasts without being overdone.

Sherise thought she dressed too conservatively and constantly bothered her about her shopping choices. Toni reminded her of this when Reecie tries to "borrow" some clothing from her that came from a shop that she thought was too "old lady". At some point, Reecie finally admitted that the clothes were well made and lasted unlike some other brands. Although smaller than Toni by a couple of sizes—she was a size 10 to Toni's 14, she often tried to abscond with some piece of Toni's clothing that would be "perfect" with something she'd picked up from a trendy, overpriced shop in Georgetown.

After putting on her makeup and adding the finishing touches to her still lasting hairdo, Toni grabbed her handbag and laptop case. Exiting through the side door into the garage, she set the alarm, let up the garage door, stepped down to her navy BMW 5-series and put her items inside. She turned the car on to get the juices flowing and walked to the edge of the curb for the morning paper. She never read the paper until it was old news, but she continued to subscribe. *Wasted money*, she thought to herself. This went totally against her frugal nature, yet she continued.

On the road to La Jolla, she thought about what she had learned on the Internet about the medical services company. The president was a former nurse who had seen a need in the medical field, and decided to do something about it. Eleven years after starting the company, Samuel Lawson had made his start-up into a thriving and profitable enterprise, a premier services company for hospitals and medical centers. In the midst of the company's success, the IT efforts became considerably less structured, resulting in some serious problems with recent releases of its software products. This is where Toni stepped in to help. She was going to propose a way to get the software development efforts under control by helping the company put processes in place that would result in the consistency the company was seeking.

Reaching the office complex that housed APEX Medical Services, Toni parked, grabbed her roller bag, and headed into the building.

APEX shared a very nice building in a complex of four other buildings. Toni proceeded to the elevator after consulting her notes from her contact within the company, Rachel Parks, the assistant to the vice president of Information Technology. Her notes indicated that she should take the elevator to the fifteenth floor.

Toni moved to the back in case others needed to board the elevator. As the elevator traveled towards the fifteenth floor, others boarded. Toni looked up from the notes she was studying to find a fine man standing in front of her. He was quite tall. There were others in the elevator, so Toni felt comfortable checking him out. *Hmm, nice hair. A little lower. Nice shoulders. A bit lower. Dang! A black man's butt, but this ain't a black man.* The navy suit pants hugged the man's butt rather nicely. *My, my, my,* she thought, running her tongue across her glossy lips. *Two fine white men in just a couple of days. Dang, they're making them finer.*

Ping! The elevator announced its arrival to the fifteenth floor.

"Excuse me," Toni spoke to the man in front of her. "This is my floor."

He moved back towards the side wall so she could pass by him. Toni looked up to say "thank you", only to realize that the man she was checking out was the same man from the coffee shop! *This would happen to me!*

"Umm, thank you," she squeezed out, while once again being embarrassed. *That butt, though. Got to admit, Girl, that he's got one butt on him.*

"You're quite welcome," he replied, with a smirk on his face. He pointed to the shiny mirrored steel in the elevator.

"Again," he said while letting one gorgeous green eye close then pop back open.

Now, there was no need for that. He's just being cheeky, Toni thought to herself as she exited the elevator without responding to his comment, but cutting her eyes at him very effectively in the way only a black woman could do. She walked towards the doors with APEX Medical Services stamped on the outside. Opening the doors, she glanced around and saw that she was in the reception area. One couldn't see what was occurring on the other side of the reception area, as there were secure badge entry doors blocking access.

"Hi. My name is Antoinette Quinn, and I'm here for a presentation today with Samuel Lawson, Jessica Adams, and Gabriel Jackson. My appointment is at nine o'clock. Rachel Parks has been my contact."

"Yes, Ms. Quinn, I have your appointment here on the calendar. Rachel is not here today, but I will get Jessica Adams for you. If you will have a seat, she will be here shortly to greet you."

"Thank you."

Toni sat down on one of the plush chocolate brown leather chairs. As she scanned the reception area, she found the area welcoming and warm. Their designer did a great job. *Wonder what the working areas look like.* In any case, Toni was cool and collected. Familiarity with making pitches to potential clients tended to calm any nervousness that wanted to arise. Clients had problems; she worked with them to come up with lasting solutions. She was establishing quite a good reputation in the process improvement and appraisal industry—for a one-woman shop that occasionally called on others to help with jobs. She was quite thankful since this was not her field of study in college.

"Ms. Quinn?"

Toni looked up to see an impeccably dressed woman with cocoa skin, deep black hair slicked into a bun, and attired in a kicking navy Armani suit, accented with a silver silk blouse with an offset drooping bow. *The sister is clean,* thought Toni.

"Yes, I'm Toni Quinn."

"I'm Jessica Adams. Nice to meet you," extending her hand in greeting, to which Toni reciprocated.

"A pleasure to meet you, too."

"We're going to go to the conference room so that you can set up. Follow me, please?" Jessica asked.

"Certainly."

Jessica swiped her badge and held the door open for Toni. Toni looked around and saw office space that was nicely configured, presumably making it a comfortable environment.

"Nice working space."

"Thank you. We try to make sure that the space is conducive to producing good work. Most of us are working long hours since our client list is steadily growing. We're hiring more employees in the next few months, so this is a good time to implement changes. Well, maybe not a good time, but any later, and we will be a way behind the curve in correcting some of our issues."

"Interesting."

"We're going to meet in the conference room on this floor. Ordinarily, we host guests in the conference room near Sam's office, but a team is using it for a video-conference with a client this morning. Sam and Gabe will be down in a bit so we can start on time."

Entering the conference room, Toni quickly surveyed the setup. SmartBoards were in place. There was what seemed to be quite comfortable seating. Wonderful.

"I'm going to go ahead and turn everything on so you can load your materials," Jessica told her.

"Thank you."

After Jessica left the conference room, Toni proceeded to prepare her materials for the presentation. She placed glossy information packets at each seat so that the client partici- pants would have something in hand before she left. She fixed herself a cup of tea from the beverage bar that was in the room after determining that she had enough time before the others arrived. As she drank her tea, she pondered that she would be working closely with the vice president of Information Technology should she get the contract. Working with a brother would not be a new experience. They were fun, but serious about the job at hand, particular- ly at this level. *Gabriel "Gabe" Jackson better have a sense of humor. If what I think is true about their way of working, he's going to have to make some tough decisions. Just what a black man needs—another woman telling him what he needs to do. Lord, he'll think I'm his mama by the time we're finished!*

Others began to arrive just as she finished her tea. Samuel Jackson came in with a smile on his face and right hand extended in greeting. She recognized him from his picture on the web site. A very good looking black man with creamy milk chocolate skin, buff but not overly muscled, he could have been a model. She quickly noticed that he wore a wedding ring and assumed that he gave plenty of private modeling sessions to his wife. *Okay, mind your business, Toni.* Several more people came in beyond those identified with Rachel via telephone, and Sam said that he would wait and introduce everyone. To her surprise and chagrin, in walked the man from the elevator and coffee shop! *I just can't escape*

Mr. Gorgeous White Man. She could feel him staring at her, but she refused to give to him the pleasure of knowing that he'd rattled her with his surprise appearance. From the look on his face, he was equally surprised.

"Okay, everybody, let's get started," Sam said as he opened the meeting. "As you know, we've had some significant product quality issues over the past year. Before this gets completely out of hand, I want to ensure that we're doing all we can to continue to provide our clients with the consistency that helped build our reputation as the best in the industry.

"To that end, I've invited Ms. Antoinette Quinn, President of Process Solutions, to talk with us about implementing some industry best practices. Welcome, Ms. Quinn." Others echoed the greeting.

"Thank you for having me."

"Before Ms. Quinn begins, I'd like each of you to introduce yourself and tell Ms. Quinn your role within the company."

As introductions were made, Toni looked at the meeting attendees, taking notes on their roles, and managing to avoid eye contact with the man from the elevator. She could feel his stare, and it was making her squirm in her seat. *It's getting a bit warm in here,* she pondered. Introductions continued, and Toni began to get a sinking feeling. The vice president of Information Technology had yet to be introduced and there were only three people left—two women and the man from the elevator. *Please do not let this be Gabriel Jackson!*

Finally, the last person introduced himself.

"My name is Gabriel Jackson," he stated rather lazily with his gorgeous smile aimed directly at Toni, for she had no escape and he knew it, since not looking at him would be the height of professional rudeness. "I am the vice president of Information Technology." The look he gave Toni was so hot she could have melted right in her chair. She could feel her nipples tightening.

Well, so much for assumptions. What have I done lately to deserve this, Toni ruefully thought, while trying to not be obvious about the piece of paper she was waving back and forth. The room was not hot at all, but the look he gave her was enough to make her think she needed some Prempro.

"Umm, Ms. Quinn, would you like to begin?" asked Sam, while looking oddly at Gabe, and passing a look at Toni who sat at one end of the table for presentation purposes. Sam and Gabe had been friends for a long time, so Sam was privy to Gabe's moods just as Gabe was with his. He knew something was amiss, but couldn't think about that right then.

"Certainly. Everyone, my name is Toni Quinn." Swallowing and standing, literally commanding her body to shut up, Toni provided the assembled group with her presentation, remembering why she was at APEX in the first place. She walked while she talked as it kept nervousness down and also served to keep the attendees alert. Tech people tended to want to do a million things at once—usually on their mobile devices—while missing critical points that she had to repeat. She found that moving around lessened the mobile device activities.

As she moved around the room, she saw and felt the steady, concentrated gaze of Gabe Jackson. When she moved past the chair opposite his, she knew he was watching her butt. *The nerve of this man*, forgetting that she had subjected him to the same thorough view of his back.

"The first thing we will do is examine what your current documented processes are, but what your undocumented habits and behaviors are, as well. This will serve as the baseline. Then we will assess which best practices will help you immediately and which ones will require additional implementation time." Toni continued with her presentation, answering questions as they arose.

"Any more questions?" she queried the group.

"Will senior management be involved in this baseline assessment?" asked Gabe, looking her directly in the eyes.

"Umm, yes, they will. I believe that senior management must be engaged in any major improvement initiative. Consequently, some time will be spent asking questions of senior management. They, too, develop habits and behaviors. Often, these habits and behaviors are transferred to their staff unknowingly."

"Hmm. I wonder what kind of habits I've developed. I'm looking forward to it," he said with a smile and totally inappropriate wink of his green eye.

Are you kidding me? she thought, while at the same time, breathing to calm the heat that suddenly consumed her body.

Since there were no more questions, Toni closed out her presentation with some hearty thanks for the group's time, totally ignoring Gabe's remark. *I'm gonna have to set him straight if he keeps this up. This is work!*

Sam thanked everyone for attending and adjourned the meeting. Toni packed up her materials while Jessica waited to walk her out. Jessica thanked her again and said that Sam would be in touch.

"Okay, we're going to hire her firm, right?" Gabe asked Sam as he walked into his office without knocking. This was not customary, while although they were very best of friends, Gabe and Sam kept things at the office very professional. It was no secret, though, amongst the staff that they were longtime friends, business partners, and had a relationship that extended beyond the office.

"Hello to you, too, Gabe. What's up with you, man?"

"Hi, Sam. Anyway, she's the one."

"She's the one what?"

"She's the one from the coffee shop."

"What coffee shop?" as Sam continued to check his email.

"Sam, would you look up and listen to me?" as he sat down in one of the brown leather chairs in front of Sam's desk, crossing one of his long legs across the other.

"Okay. One moment," as he closed the last email. He was attempting to stay on top of the deluge of email he received daily.

"Ms. Antoinette Quinn is the woman I told you about on Saturday."

"She was the one in the coffee shop? Ms. Quinn? Are you sure?" Sam asked, looking skeptical.

"Not just the coffee shop. I saw her doing it again this morning on the elevator. She didn't move a lot, but I could see her in the side mirrors. I sort of called her on it, but she played it off like nothing happened and that she didn't recognize me."

"Evidently the woman has a fetish or a problem. And you want me to hire her?"

"Sure do. The sooner the better."

"Why? What are you planning to do?"

"Marry her."

"Marry her? You don't know her."

"Not yet, but I will."

"Okaaayyy. What has happened to my normally re-served friend Gabriel? You are Gabe Jackson, right?"

"Yeah. She's the one, though. Remember how you felt when you met Denni? I feel like that. I said to myself on

Saturday that if I met her again, I would ask her out. This is "again"."

"No, this morning on the elevator was "again". You want us to pay this woman a hefty fee just so you can ask her out and get your feelings hurt by a black woman who, while cordial, doesn't act like she plays the radio? Are you crazy?"

"Not one bit."

"Okay. I know my lovely wife Denni cooked you a great meal on Sunday, but did you get food poisoning? I'm going to call your mama. That will wake you up. Heck, it took her five visits and my grandmama's peach cobbler to get her used to our being friends. Wonder what she'll say about you and a black woman. Anyway, now, I can't get rid of your mother. By the way, she wants you to call her. Why your mama calls me to tell you to call her is beyond me."

"I have to see her again, Sam."

"Did you see that woman in there? She is a professional all the way through. There is no way she's going to date a client, man. Forget it."

"So, we're going to hire her, huh?"

"Gabe, are you sure? You're going to have to work with her a lot. What if it doesn't work out?"

"Sam, we've been friends for a long time. Trust me on this. I know we've heard from other firms, but I want us to hire her firm, okay?"

Sam looked at him. He sensed that his friend and business partner was completely set on hiring Toni Quinn's firm. They were partners in the firm, although the positions were different. Gabe bought into the business when he came on as the vice president for Information Technology and was looking for an investment opportunity.

"Okay. We may as well. I guess I should get some excellent advice and help while you're trying out for the Next Great Fool to Fall in Lust."

"Good. See you later. We're still on for dinner tonight, right?"

"Yes. Come early. I got things I wanna do with Denni tonight, if you know what I mean."

"TMI."

Chapter 4

"Denni, your son is here!" Sam loudly proclaimed after opening the door to Gabe. His wife Denise "Denni" Reems-Lawson was in the kitchen cooking. Gabe usually dined with them at least once a week. Ever since meeting Gabe back when she and Sam were dating and seeing the close relationship between her future husband and the reserved white man, Denni had made it a mission to ensure he always felt included and to loosen him up. She'd done a good job.

"Honey, I'm home!" Gabe called out just as loudly, while heading straight to the kitchen to greet Denni.

Denni was standing at the stove. Gabe walked up, put his arms around her, gave her a kiss on her neck—her spot for her husband, but not a flicker when Gabe mimicked Sam, and both men knew it—and whispered somewhat loudly, "What do you see in him? Baby, I can take you away from all this. Wanna go?"

"Umm, hmm. Right after I feed him. He needs to be very full in order to prevent his immediate chase and capture of the very unwise man who would attempt to carry me away. I'm all that, you know. He'd miss me in five minutes—guaranteed."

"Two minutes—max," Sam noted, walking into the kitchen. "By the way, why are you always kissing on my wife, man?"

"'Cause I can, and she doesn't care. She's secretly in love with me, and I with her."

"Just this morning you were proclaiming that you were going to marry the new consultant. Now, it's my wife?" Sam jokingly replied. "He's fickle, sweetheart. You best stay with me. You may find yourself outdoors in no time."

Walking away from the stove, patting Gabe's face on the way, Denni put her arms around her husband's neck, placed every body part that she could right flush against his, and told him in her sexiest bedroom voice, "Tonight, I'm going to show you just how much I want to stay with you. Make sure you eat plenty. You're going to need all the energy you can get."

"Are y'all trying to make me jealous?" asked Gabe.

"No, but I would like you to get a to-go box!" Sam responded, while leaning down to give his wife a kiss.

"Gabe, grab the dishes and set the table, please. Sam, would you grab something to drink, please?" Denni laughingly ordered as she went back to the stove, swinging her hips for the benefit of her one and only husband of three years.

She marveled at the relationship between the two men. Having met in college more than twenty years ago, the men were still as close as brothers. They'd been through it all—girlfriends, fiancées, skeptical parents, siblings, relatives, and colleagues. Yet, they remained close, occasionally going to the wall one for the other. As a black woman from a small East Coast town, she was in awe of their bond.

"Gabe, what is this about you wanting to marry a consultant?" Denni asked after Sam had blessed the food and they began to eat the roast, vegetables, and potatoes prepared by Denni.

"Do you want to tell her, or should I?" Sam prodded his friend.

"I can speak for myself, thank you very much," Gabe answered Sam. "Denni, I met this woman, and it turns out she is the president of the firm we interviewed today to help with our development issues."

"What's unusual about that?" Denni asked, turning her head towards Sam.

"Do you want to tell her, or should I?" Sam prodded again.

"Go ahead. You can't sit still from wanting to reveal," Gabe told him without rancor.

"Saturday, your dear friend Gabe found himself getting checked out in the coffee shop by this woman. He called her on it. She didn't realize he could see her in the mirror behind the counter. This morning, Gabe caught her at it again in the office building elevator. Apparently, Gabe has an eye-catching rear. It turns out the woman checking him out is the same *sistah* we interviewed this morning for the improvement initiative. He claims she's the one."

"She's black?" Denni inquired, with one eyebrow raised.

"Yes, Antoinette Quinn is black, tall, shapely, and completely unlike any woman Gabe has ever dated."

"Gabe?" Denni asked. She was surprised, as the only women Gabe had dated as long as she'd known him were white women—petite, brunette, smart, and eager to head to the altar. Such eagerness, however, had not propelled her very handsome, caring friend to say "I do". To hear this news about Antoinette Quinn was definitely unexpected and yes, somewhat amusing.

"I don't know, Denni. She moves me. I don't mean just physically, although, I have to tell you watching and listening to her today made me want to clear the room. I haven't had more than a few minutes' conversation with her, but I know that I have to get to know her. So, Sam is going to issue a contract to her for the work."

"Whoa. You're hiring her firm because you want to get to know her? Why not just ask her out?" Denni asked.

"I don't know how she feels about dating a white man. Besides, I don't know when I would get another chance. San Diego is rather widespread, and I may not get to see her again. So, I'm seizing the opportunity. Offering her the contract is not a favor; she knows her stuff, and I think we'll be well-pleased with her help. And, it gives me plenty of time to get to know her and she me," Gabe told her, with a twinkle in his green eyes.

"I think you're serious," Denni told him.

"I am, Denni. Very serious."

"Sam? What do you think, honey?" Denni asked of her husband.

"I think he's got his work cut out for him. Ms. Quinn doesn't look like she has much patience for foolishness. She doesn't seem mean, but you can tell she is about work when it's work. She has to be; she's a one-woman shop. A very impressive client list, but she didn't get that list by being lax about business. You're going to have to work hard to interject any personal moments, Gabe. I hope you're ready. Sistahs can cut without even trying."

"What is that supposed to mean?" Denni saucily asked him.

"Umm… sweetheart, no offense, but you know and I know that a black woman can cut deep, and keep walking like she'd offered a slice of cherry pie. I'm just saying that as a white man who has never dated a black woman, he should be prepared."

"But I know plenty of black women. Denni, your mother—and Lord knows your dad has his hands full with Mrs. Sarah—and especially, your sisters."

"But you know them socially. You haven't dated them, tried to get close to them, tried…oh, forget it. I'm going to sit back and watch the drama unfold. I hope you're ready, man."

"I am. If she's half as good a woman as your Denise, then I'd be pleased."

"Whaaaatt? You wanna take some food home, huh?" Denni joyously and pleasantly asked after the very sincere compliment.

"Baby, baby, baby," Gabe sang in a good Barry White imitation. "Antoinette who?"

Gabe knew that Sam was simply concerned. He didn't want to see Sam get hurt. After so many years as friends, Gabe and Sam alike had experienced their share of women-gone-wrong. At thirty-nine years of age, both men had dated any number of women. Sam had been engaged before he met Denni, only to have the woman cheat on him with a colleague of Sam's during the time he was a nurse. They very carefully watched the women who came into their lives. He hoped that she had her act together, as neither he nor Sam handled foolish women that well.

When Sam met Denni five years ago, it took Gabe quite a while before he knew she was serious about guarding the heart of his friend. Since then, he'd fallen in love with her—respectfully, of course—and wondered if he would meet someone equally as willing to share his life as Denni did Sam's. A senior accountant with a local firm, she worked a very busy schedule but still tried to cook a meal at least twice per week, which was something they had discussed before getting married. On the other days, Sam cooked, or they had dinner out. It was a partnership in the truest sense of the word. They also had plenty of passion which hadn't seemed to abate since they married. If anything, they seemed to enjoy each other more and more. This is what Gabe had come to want within the past year.

Truthfully, he had not envisioned marrying at this point. He was well aware that he was an attractive male—physically, socially, and financially. He dated, but had become quite selective in the past year, preferring his own company or that of his family and friends to that of an ambitious woman looking to hang up her career for the title of "wife", specifically, "Mrs. Gabriel Jackson". Watching Sam and Denni had raised the bar, so to speak, on his expectations in a wife and for married life.

Antoinette Quinn, you better have more going for you than a luscious body, agile mind, and solid career. I need more. I need you to be emotionally secure, spiritually stable, and just plain solid.

Just thinking of Toni's luscious body had Gabe squirming in the seat of his silver Lexus SUV. *I've got to taste her.* He wondered how long it would be before his curiosity about Toni was satisfied. In the meantime, he supposed his multi-spray shower was waiting for him—with cold water all the way.

Chapter 5

His long finger stroked her collarbone, moving down her shoulder to trace a sensuous path down her arm. The surveying of the landscape of her body continued with a trek on the underside of her arm and over to her luscious breasts. Teasingly, the finger tapped the tip of her breast, but did not linger, putting the recipient in a state of frustration. Her nipple cried out for attention, but its hunger would not be appeased.

The finger continued its trip down the right side of her body, tracing the indenture of her waist, the fullness of the hips the finger's owner loved, the long legs that held him captivated, only to increase the frustration of the recipient by tracing up the inside of that leg, the thigh and alighting upon her core.

"Gabe!" Toni's breath hitched. "What are you doing to me?"

"What your husband has a right to do. Loving you the best way I know how."

"Don't stop," she begged squirming on the bed, "Please don't stop."

"No worries, Mrs. Jackson," he responded in a voice thick with passion, as he continued with his survey. "I'm not stopping anytime soon."

"Mmm—"

"The weather in San Diego is a cool forty-nine degrees this morning and reaching a high of around sixty-eight. We expect clear skies and plenty of sunshine," the radio jockey announced in his way too perky voice for six-thirty in the morning.

Toni sat straight up in bed, breathing hard, sweating, and wondering if she had indeed been having sex with Gabe—as her husband no less! The dream seemed so real. Her blood was racing, her breathing was labored, and she was very conspicuously wet. *Oh, my goodness. What have I gotten myself into? A white man? Married? This is not the way to start my first day with APEX. All day, I will be thinking about this dream.*

Arising from the bed, Toni noticed that her short peach silk gown was sticking to her body. *I need a shower. Apparently, that's not all I need,* she joked to herself, thinking about how her love juices flowed from just a dream.

The concentration on her work life did not leave a lot of room for relationships. A short relationship earlier in her career ended badly, so she made a decision to not even bother. Years had passed since Toni had dated seriously, or wanted to for that matter, and to find herself with the hots for a white man did not fall in line with her plans.

Sure, she desired to meet someone who would see her as a partner, but she had not crossed many in her walk of life. She also wanted children, but was unwilling to go the route so many of her contemporaries were taking. Successful women were deciding to have children without husbands since it seemed that husband material was in short demand. Toni thought this was partially true; she recognized that women played a role, too.

Some women had an unwillingness to consider men who did not meet their degree requirements, salary expectations, and a host of other qualities—keeping otherwise eligible men out of the running. These women were missing out on men—those who would work hard, remain faithful, and just be good men, husbands and fathers.

Toni did not agree with the thinking of these women; she just did not have time for foolishness and in reality, taking chances. She liked a sure bet, and she had come to realize that there was no such thing where men were concerned.

After her shower, Toni stood in her robe viewing the contents of the walk-in for something to catch her eye. Getting dressed today was easier since the environment was business casual. Her gaze landed on an attractive, red surplice sweater. With the right bra, her breasts would sit nicely rounded, showing enough cleavage to be attractive but not unprofessional. Saying "I'm confident, and these are *mine*, but I'm not a hussy," basically. She paired the sweater with a pair of off-white trousers. Adding black patent leather pumps and a black patent leather belt, she was set for the day. Dressy enough to convey the impression of an expert at work, but comfortable enough to make it through the day without wishing she had worn something else.

Before dressing, Toni went to the kitchen to grab a bite to eat. Normally not a breakfast eater, Toni decided that today she needed fortification before heading to work. She grabbed a bowl for some grain cereal and almond milk. While she puttered around the kitchen fixing breakfast, she flipped on the under-the-counter stereo system on what came on was Kirk Franklin's "I Like Me". She sang loud and proud with the song. She liked this anthem of self-love, self-like that stated that it didn't matter whether anyone else liked you, but you sure better like yourself.

After eating cereal and having an invigorating cup of tea, Toni returned to her bedroom to dress. Clothes, makeup, hair—she was ready. After the usual ritual of leaving the house, Toni was on the highway heading to APEX and pondering how the day would go. After an initial, prearranged meeting with the development team later in the morning, Toni would begin the process of reviewing current practices and operations. This could be time-consuming. Since the contract was not for an indefinite length of time, but with very specific goals, Toni had no time to waste, so efficiency was the order of the day.

Upon arrival, one of the office assistants showed her to her space. She had been assigned a full office with a door, which was indeed a surprise. She would keep the door open when she was not out "on the floor" with the development team. She often worked side-by-side with staff so that she could better understand their work habits.

Settled in her office at APEX, Toni was not logged on to her computer for more than a few minutes when she sensed someone in the doorway. Looking up, it was none other than Gabe Jackson, looking so good that she felt her body temperature take an immediate spike. He was dressed rather handsomely in a navy dress shirt with French cuffs and links, tan pants, along with a brown alligator belt and shoes. *Dang, he even dresses well. Of course, you already knew this, Toni.*

"Good morning. May I help you?" she inquired in a voice that was surprisingly steady considering she had just experienced a flashback from that morning's dream.

"Good morning, Ms. Quinn. I came by to see if you were properly settled and if anything was needed. I want you to be as comfortable as possible while you're here at APEX."

"Please, call me Toni. To answer your question, I'm settled just fine, thank you. It is nice to arrive at a client site and everything is ready to go. Network connections, telephone, etc. Please thank your team for the effort. It is greatly appreciated."

"Our pleasure," in a voice that indicated he considered "pleasure" to be more than she had stated.

"Is there anything else?" Toni asked with her hands poised over her computer, a clear indicator that she wanted to cut this impromptu visit short before she melted in her seat.

"Yes, I'd like to discuss a few things with you before you get started and have this morning's kickoff meeting."

"Certainly. Please come in and have a seat."

Stepping across the threshold and closing the door, Gabe turned around to catch Toni with one eyebrow raised at this closing of the door.

"Habit. Sorry," Gabe said so insincerely, that Toni knew it really was not habit but he was taking advantage of the situation.

"I keep the door open unless there is something of a sensitive nature that needs to be discussed. For future reference, of course," she stated firmly.

"Certainly," Gabe stated, borrowed her oft-used word.

"So…"

"So, since you will be here for the next few months working with the teams that are in my organization, I wanted to assure you that you have my full support. If there are any issues with cooperation, please come see me."

"First, while I appreciate the offer, if there are any issues, I will first seek to resolve them with the individual. If not, then with the manager in charge. Lastly, with you if there is no resolution. I don't want the team to think that I am here as a spy. I am not. I am here to help determine how they're working and how some changes can help the organization meet its goals of fewer problems with released software. That and that alone."

"Okaayy. Quite the professional, aren't you? We are somewhat relaxed here, so you know. We are all very busy, and we find that keeping things a bit light helps to balance things out, if you will. In any case, should you need me, call me—anytime. Here is my card with my office and cellular phone numbers. Also, after this morning's meeting, I would like to invite you to lunch to find out your first impressions. I assume you are free."

"I am free; however, lunch today is not an option. I'd like to spend the time solidifying the plan of approach so that we can get started right away. I assume you are okay with the schedule I sent to you and your leads last week?"

"I am, but I really would like to have lunch today. I am on travel beginning Wednesday through the rest of the work week, so I would like to touch base before I leave."

"Hmm. How is tomorrow?"

"Not possible. Ms. Quinn—Toni—is lunch a problem?"

"Umm, no, it is not a problem, just not desirable today."

"Thank you for being so frank," he stated with a smirk. "I will come for you at twelve fifteen."

"Fine," Toni stated in a very reluctant and unprofessional voice.

"And, Toni?"

"Yes?" as she looked up.

"Let's start over. I will completely ignore the fact that we met under different circumstances. Okay? No harm done."

Toni's eyes squinted, and she had to catch herself before she told him off in no uncertain terms. To even bring up the incidents was unprofessional, in her opinion. She was all set to forget that the events had occurred. To her advantage, of course, since she had not known that the object of her inspection would be her next client. For said client to bring up the matter was just—well, aggravating!

"Certainly, Mr. Jackson," she told him frostily.

"Feisty, too," he muttered with a smile crossing his lips.

"Excuse me?" Toni asked, hearing his comment.

"Nothing. Toni, my name is Gabe. Just call me Gabe. I'll see you shortly at the meeting and again for lunch. Thanks for being so accommodating," he told her in parting shot.

He knew she could do lunch today, but for some reason she was dodging. He assumed it was due to their prior encounters, unintended though they were. *Well, too bad. Maybe she'll stop going around town and checking out strange men.* He had an agenda, and he did not plan to wait until she was comfortable. After this conversation, he realized that getting to know her may not be so easy unless he got a surprise. *Wouldn't that be something?* He guessed that had his work cut out for him. He could go the distance, but he needed to get to know her first. So, lunch today would be the start.

Toni was positively seething after Gabe left her office. *The nerve of this man to just assume that I have time to stop what I'm doing and have lunch!* The still-sane part of her responded with, *Toni, you know this is a client. Just because you're having a reaction to him does not mean you can avoid the normal client interactions. You know that you normally do lunch with a client within the first few days of the contract. Why the change? Get over it.* Toni decided to yield to the sensible part of her.

The rest of the morning went as planned. The kickoff meeting with the development team—comprised of smaller team such as requirements, infrastructure, programming, test, deployment, and support—went very well. For the most part, everyone was receptive with the plan of approach. The goals were clearly identified and all knew that they were expected to help accomplish those goals by being forthcoming during interview sessions and working sessions.

Lunch time loomed. Toni was in her office documenting meeting notes for distribution to the team when the call came.

"This is Toni Quinn."

"Toni, Gabe here. I'm sorry, but may I change our time to twelve-thirty instead of twelve-fifteen? I'm in conference with a client, and we should be finished by then."

"Certainly."

"Hmm. Do your "certainlies" really mean "certainly", or is that just your way of not saying what you'd really rather say?" Gabe asked.

"I thought you were in a teleconference?" Toni responded.

"You're right. Anyway, ponder your answer, and you can share it during lunch," Gabe retorted.

"Certainly."

"Touché. See you at twelve-thirty, and thanks."

Toni looked at the receiver in her hand and once again wondered she had gotten herself into with this contract.

Gabe walked to the other end of the building in order to retrieve his lunch date. He knew she would probably take offense at calling this business meeting a "lunch date". He smiled inwardly while greeting employees. The IT department was medium-sized, around one hundred sixty staff members, split between the office locations. Gabe was the vice president, but he knew what it meant to be on the other side and had not forgotten the long hours that development teams put in so that products went out on time. He had been an employee and consultant at various times throughout his career. The latter made it possible to buy into APEX and partner with Sam. Consequently, he tried to ensure that the environment was conducive to producing the work that was necessary to keep the company going and the client list growing.

Reaching Toni's office, Gabe tapped on the wood of the doorframe to announce his arrival.

Toni looked up from her computer. She was on the phone at the same time. She held up a finger while she completed her call. He listened to her call.

"Hmm, mmm. I look forward to seeing you, too."

Toni smiled between comments.

"Yes, Alex. I love you, too. Bye, Love."

Toni clicked off her cell phone, locked her computer, reached into her desk and grabbed her handbag. "I'm ready," she told Gabe who was looking at her weirdly. "Is something wrong?"

"No, nothing's wrong. Let's go."

"Okay," she responded somewhat quizzically.

They walked through the office space, past reception, and to the elevator. When they boarded, it was empty. Gabe asked how the rest of her morning had gone and she inquired about his. The stilted chitchat ceased as other passengers boarded, making it necessary for Gabe to move closer to her.

Oh, he smells so good.

What fragrance is she wearing? I need to buy stock in the company.

I hope I make it through lunch without acting crazy.

I hope I make it through lunch without scaring her.

The elevator announced its arrival. They and the other passengers disembarked. They walked to his SUV parked in the office building garage. Gabe and Toni were both happy to be released from the elevator. Such close quarters were working havoc with both their libidos.

When they reached the truck, Gabe opened the door for Toni and helped her up, both catching their breaths as Toni's breast brushed against Gabe's arm, causing immediate, visible proof of the chemistry between them. Gabe walked to the driver's side, pausing to take a deep breath. After starting the car, Gabe told Toni where they were dining. There was a nice seafood restaurant near the beach that he liked and thought she would, too.

"I'm sorry; I should've asked. Are you allergic to seafood?"

Toni laughed, glad for the reprieve from the sexual tension. "Ah, no, I'm not allergic to seafood. I'm from Florida and adore seafood. That isn't to say that there aren't Floridians who are allergic—I know some—I just don't happen to be one of them."

"Wonderful." He paused. "Would it offend you if I told you that you look absolutely lovely today?"

"No, it would not. Thank you. You look quite nice yourself."

"Thank you," Gabe responded, somewhat surprised that she would make such a personal comment. Sam had proven to be right about her being all about business.

Gabe turned on the radio to the local jazz station. As they made their way to the restaurant, Gabe asked about her first impressions. She told him what she thought. No surprises for him, but he was quite impressed by her keen observations in so short a period. Evidently, she had spent part of the morning visiting with personnel before and after the kickoff meeting, polling them about their thoughts. She had gone right to work upon arrival. They had made a good decision by hiring her if this was any indication of the caliber of her work.

Once at the restaurant, Gabe parked. He walked around to Toni's side, only to find that she was already alighting from the vehicle. Gabe closed the door behind her and pressed the remote lock.

"Toni, I can do that."

"Do what?"

"Open your door, help you down."

"Oh, can you?" she said warningly while he was totally unaware that he had stepped into a hornet's nest.

"Yes, I can. Gentlemen do, you know."

"I—," Toni gasped, completely ending her about-to-be dress down. Gabe had reached behind her and touched her back as a guide to the restaurant. Toni literally felt electricity move from his hand to her body. All of a sudden every body part stood at attention from the shock. She peeked over at Gabe, who still had his hand at her back. His jaw was tight, and his green eyes had darkened considerably; she could see this as he glanced down at her. He had felt it, too.

"Toni, just walk, please. No talking, okay?"

"Sure, but—"

"Unless you don't want lunch today, please no talking until we're seated. Okay?" he gritted out through clenched teeth.

Toni wisely kept her mouth close. *I'm in trouble.*

Reaching the hostess stand, Gabe stood close behind her. She could feel the heat rolling off his body. *Oh, I'm in so much trouble. Help me make it through lunch.* This had gone from business to personal in a quantum leap. She had a flashback from this morning's dream, and her body temperature spiked again. *I need a drink of something really cold, really fast.*

"Gabriel Jackson. Two for lunch, please."

The hostess consulted her reservations and said, "Right this way, Mr. Jackson."

As soon as they were seated and the server came over to greet them, Toni said, "I'd like a glass of ice water, please."

"I would like one, as well, please," Gabe requested, looking at her like she was going to be lunch. *This woman has me tied up and I don't even know her.*

"Right away. Please take a few minutes to review the menu," replied the server before walking away.

Returning with their glasses of water, he noticed that the menus had not been opened.

"Sir? Ma'am?" Receiving no answer, he said, "I'll give you a few more minutes."

They both nodded their heads while looking at each other so intensely, the server abruptly turned away. A good thing they were in a secluded booth. If they had not been, the other patrons would have been the recipient of looks so hot that their seafood could have been steamed all over again.

"Gabe?"

"Yes, Toni?"

"Umm. Is it okay to talk now?"

Gabe swallowed a drink of water before speaking. "Toni, I'd rather that we order lunch, eat, and then go. I am this close"—pinching his thumb and index fingers together with just a hair of separation—"to calling off lunch. Okay?"

"Okay."

When the server returned, he received the response lacking from his prior visit. Toni ordered steamed shrimp, snapper, and vegetables. Gabe ordered a half lobster, steamed crab legs, and the steamed vegetables. By mutual unspoken consent, they opted not to have an appetizer. It would only prolong the torture. As it was, Gabe's eyes tried to stay focused somewhere over Toni's shoulder, around the restaurant, or beyond the window where the beach was across the highway. Anywhere but on Toni's breasts with nipples in stark relief. He knew she knew they were extended since she was blushing and kept trying to position her arms in such a way to hide her arousal. After a few minutes, he knew he had to give her a way to deal with things.

"Toni?"

"Yes, Gabe?"

"I didn't bring you to lunch to make you feel uncomfortable, but I want to be honest with you. I am *very* attracted to you. I want to get to know you. I believe you feel the same way."

"Gabe, I don't mix business with pleasure. It's a bad recipe. Equally important, I do not date white men."

"You don't date white men? What does my being white have to do with anything?"

"I'm strictly chocolate, Gabe. Please don't be offended," Toni said.

"Strictly chocolate?" Gabe laughed. "What is that?"

"I only date black men."

"What? Really?" he asked in disbelief.

"Yes."

"Hmm. I would think a woman with such broad experience would think differently about such things."

"You don't know me well enough to make such a statement," Toni snapped.

"You're right," he conceded due to the crispness of her voice. "My apologies, please."

"Hmm. Apology accepted," she replied somewhat grudgingly.

"Well, I'm proposing that we get to know each other. I am simply asking if you're willing to explore this attraction."

"I'm not going to act like I don't know what you're talking about. I am attracted to you, but acting on the attraction is something different. I don't date white men, Gabe. I'm sorry, but that is just the way it is."

"I'm asking that you reconsider your stance. I'm asking if you're willing to explore this attraction that we both feel—outside of the office. At work, it will be all business."

"All business, huh? Gabe, let me ask you a question. How will this look to Sam, the other executives, and to the staff? Apart from which, I hadn't planned on dating a white man."

"As for Sam and the other executives, I don't see a problem, as you're not an employee, you're a supplier. As for the latter, I wish you would reconsider. I'm a good guy. Really," he said, winking his eye.

"I just never envisioned dating a white man. There are lots of issues associated with cross-cultural dating."

"I get it. Sam and I were roommates in college and quickly became rather inseparable. Not everyone, including my family initially, understood the bond that developed between us. So, I get it. But, this is us. Let's start and see if we're interested in continuing before we borrow trouble, okay?"

"I don't know, Gabe. What if we start, continue down the road, and find that things don't work out? I am under contract with APEX, and no matter how attracted to you I am, work comes first. I'm not willing to work in a tense atmosphere because of a romance-gone-bad."

"Let's try, Toni, okay?"

Toni did not respond to Gabe's query right way, but instead concentrated on her seafood which the server had just delivered. Both began to eat. After several more minutes of silence, Toni put down her fork and took a swallow of water.

Toni told Gabe, "I have absolutely no idea why I'm agreeing to this. I keep thinking, though, that if I do not try this, I am going to miss something. So, I'm willing. Please don't make me regret my decision. Whether this thing between us survives the contract or not, I will not have my business reputation put into jeopardy. If it does survive, fine. If it doesn't, you better act just like it never began, and I'll do the same. You are an executive, and how you are perceived by your staff is equally, if not more, important to me."

Gabe had to admire a woman who considered not just her own reputation, but was also willing to consider his. It did not matter so much for him since he was part owner of the company, but he understood her concern, as well.

He raised his glass of water and stated, "I propose a toast." Toni raised her glass, looking at him oddly. "To the exploration of this attraction. May it bring much pleasure."

He gave Toni a look filled with such wanting that she did not take the time to agree. She gulped the rest of her water and set the glass back on the table.

"Gabe, may I suggest we take this slow?"

"You may, but I'm not making any guarantees."

That summarily shut her up again. All these silences from Toni were very uncommon. She was well known for not mincing words and having plenty to say—sometimes when there was nothing left to say.

They continued their meal in a reflective yet comfortable silence. This was a major step for both. Gabe had never dated anyone he'd worked with, so while he was eager to see where things would lead, the decision to pursue Toni and these feelings made him stop and think. Supplier or not, he was an executive for the company for which her firm supplied services. The relationship could easily be misconstrued on all fronts, if one decided to do so.

They finished their meal, Gabe paid for the meal using his personal card, since business was not discussed except in the truck on the way to the restaurant. Toni allowed him to help her from her seat in the booth and as Gabe walked behind her with his hand on her back, he leaned over and whispered to her, "You smell wonderful."

Toni immediately experienced another hot flash. Maybe she needed to go see her doctor. This man could not be playing her body like a yo-yo.

"It's Cashmere Mist by Donna Karan."

"I'll keep that in mind."

When they reached the car, Gabe unlocked the vehicle, opened the passenger door, and helped Toni inside. He walked around and sat in the driver's seat. He did not start the engine, however. He turned towards Toni and told her, "I must kiss you. Please."

Toni didn't answer, just leaned over to offer herself to him for there was no need to play coy. They were past that with the acknowledged mutual attraction. He met her over the console, touched his lips to hers, and they both forgot the world outside. Gabe's kiss was firm yet teasing. He licked at her lips, not caring that they had both just consumed seafood. He had to have *her*. After several minutes, Gabe's tongue teased the opening of Toni's lips, seeking entrance to the oral passage. Without hesitation, Toni opened up while Gabe's hands reached for Toni's head, sinking his fingers into her hair. He dared not touch any other part of her body.

Gabe's tongue swept inside, moving in strong bold strokes showing her how he planned to love her if given the chance. Toni retaliated in kind, showing him that she was no shrinking violet where passion was concerned, although she had a rule about sex that she had yet to share with him. For the moment, however, she let him know that she was all woman—all woman that was all about him in that moment.

The kiss would have continued indefinitely except a patron pulling into the restaurant parking lot lightly tapped his horn in courteous warning. Gabe pulled back slowly, and Toni did the same. His breathing was labored and his body was more than a little uncomfortable. Toni's body was in total meltdown from the heated kiss. *Oh, my,* she thought, *if he kisses like this I am in BIG trouble. I wonder if he's ever had panties tossed at him?* Inwardly, she laughed because she was wearing trousers and getting to her panties would allow Gabe to see way more than she planned at this point in the budding whatever-this-thing-was between them. She also knew that Gabe would be shocked but would probably drive her to the nearest hotel to see what else she was willing to remove. This instant combustion had never overtaken Toni before—ever. It was a bit scary. A logical woman like her planned out her life, and spontaneous attraction to this man simply was not accounted for in those plans.

Gabe wondered what was going through Toni's mind. He sat in his seat trying to calm down. He glanced at her from the side of his eye and saw a thoughtful frown in her forehead. He would reach over and smooth it out, but one touch and she would be across the console and his lap. It just wouldn't do for the vice president of a well-known local company to be seen in the parking lot of a seafood restaurant having a very public afternoon rendezvous. Sam would surely kill him, his parents would be embarrassed, and his sisters would wonder who could drive their normally reserved brother to such a PDA (public display of affection). If only they knew.

He took a deep breath, started the vehicle, and told Toni, "I could say I'm sorry things got out of hand, but I'd be lying. I've wanted to kiss you since you showed up at our offices for proposals. During your initial presentation, you were looking like you were all business, even after getting caught on the elevator. All I could think while you were giving that presentation was, *I wonder what her lips taste like.* Now, I know."

"I thought we weren't going to mention that again," Toni teasingly and breathlessly replied, letting him know that everything was okay.

Gabe laughed, relieved that she was okay. "You're right. I did promise that, didn't I?"

Toni reached over and patted his leg, "That's okay. You're allowed this one slip."

Gabe grabbed her hand before she could remove it. A mistake, he quickly realized, since his body had yet to recover from the kiss and he could feel blood rushing back to his center. Before their extended lunch became really extended and raised eyebrows, Gabe lifted Toni's hand and placed it back in her lap.

"Umm, we better go," he told her.

"You're right."

Although it seemed that much time had passed since they had left the office, they had only been gone a respectable hour and forty-five minutes. The restaurant was only fifteen minutes away, but it was also a couple of communities over and pricier than some of the regular lunch haunts, lessening the chance of anyone seeing them, planned by Gabe with absolutely no idea of how things would end up between the two of them.

When they reached the parking garage, Gabe turned off the car and looked at Toni. She looked like she had been thoroughly kissed, which she had, but he decided not to share that with her. She had repaired her lipstick in the truck's visor mirror, so he assumed she was aware. Maybe she didn't get the full effect; he sure did, and it made him want to start all over again. *Okay, time to shut down all engines. Nothing is happening today, so just be quiet,* he ruefully told himself.

"Toni?"

"Yes?"

"I'll call you tonight. I'm busy the rest of the afternoon, but I'll call you, okay?"

"No problem, Gabe."

"I know it's not a problem, but I want you to know that I'll call you and that I'm serious."

"Okay. Do you have my cell phone number? It's on my card."

"Yes, I have it," he responded, not telling her that it was already programmed into his phone and assigned its own speed dial number. She would think he was crazy, and possibly be half right. He smiled to himself.

"What's so funny?"

"I'll let you know one day."

"Secrets? You're entitled," she told him teasingly yet seriously.

"Not a secret, but it's just not for right now."

He leaned over, kissed her on the cheek, tapped her on the nose and said, "Let's go. We both have work to do."

"Certainly."

Gabe laughed as he helped her out of the truck, locked the vehicle, and surreptitiously adjusted himself. *No need to let everyone know how good his "lunch date" had been,* he thought.

They walked into the building, rode the elevator, stepped through the secured doors behind the reception area, told each other "thank you for a nice lunch", and went about the rest of the day. Neither realized that each wore a smile that was not the ordinary "I had a good lunch with my colleague" smile. Oh, well. Maybe, it was the start of something new.

Chapter 6

Toni made it home after a very good, if surprising, first day with APEX. If anyone had told her that she would agree to date a client, a white man at that, Toni would have vehemently denied such a thing. But, she had, and she eagerly anticipated his phone call that evening.

She decided to shower, throw together a meal, call her parents, and start reading a novel she had been intending to get to for the past week. After showering and throwing on some loungewear, Toni clipped her cell phone to her waist and called her parents while she prepared her dinner. It was getting late on the east coast, but like her and her siblings, her parents were night owls. Not as late as when they were younger, but ten o'clock would find them wide awake and sometimes even midnight. Of course, Toni avoided calling so late out of respect for their privacy and age.

Her mom answered the phone as usual. Toni declared her mother sat near the telephone. She loved to talk on the phone. She talked to her parents who were still living, her siblings, her in-laws, friends—anybody and everybody.

"Hi, Ma. This is Toni."

"Hey, Baby. I know it's you."

"How're you doing? Are you feeling better?" Her mother had been dealing with a slight attack of allergies. Springtime in Florida stirred up lots of things that could bother the respiratory system.

"I'm better. Your daddy has been playing nurse, so you know how that's been," Regina laughingly told her. "I've had to un-doctor myself so that I could get well."

"Now, Ma, he's not that bad. Is he?"

"Child, your daddy could make a dead man wish he were dead by the time he finished with all his concoctions!"

Toni heard her daddy say something in the background which sounded like, "You're better, aren't you?"

"Yes, dear, I'm better," she told him.

Toni laughed. She could tell they were up to their usual jokes. Darryl and Regina were well known for their jokes about each other. After all these years, perhaps their ability to laugh together, at one another, and at themselves helped them stay together. *Hmm. Something to ponder,* Toni thought.

"Ma, let me speak to Daddy, please."

"Sure. Darryl, your daughter wants to speak to you."

"Hi, Pumpkin. How are things?"

"Things are fine. How are you? Enjoying your car?"

"Ah, your uncle and I took it for a spin. You know we were doing about ninety miles an hour. It was one smooth ride, I tell you."

"Did y'all get stopped and ticketed?" Her father and uncles were notoriously fast drivers, who had taught their children how to drive fast, too, only to complain when they received tickets.

"No ticket this time, Pumpkin."

"Daddy, I'm thirty-six. Why are you still calling me Pumpkin?" she teased him.

"The same reason I still call Reecie "Sugarplum" and Alex "Baby Boy". You are my children, and I completely reserve the right to call you what I want as long as it's respectful."

"Okay, Daddy. I was just asking, you know." Each year they had this conversation about nicknames. He was prone to calling them out at inappropriate times. Toni remembered meeting friends in high school and having her dad call out, "Call me when you're ready, Pumpkin!" That habit had stretched right on into her thirties, unfortunately. Still, they let him do it out of love.

"Everything all right out there? You met anybody, Pumpkin?"

"Umm, that's usually Mom's territory, isn't it?"

"Who do you think tells her to ask these things? I need a grandchild to ride shotgun in that Porsche, you know."

"Daddy, our family is so large if you need a kid to ride shotgun, I'll have one ready tomorrow and three on standby!" she told him.

"Girl, don't make me get on a plane and come to San Diego. And, you didn't answer my question."

"I may have met someone. It's just at the beginning stages," Toni told Darryl.

"So, you're talking? Is that it?"

Talking and a bit more, Daddy, but no need to share that with you!

"Yes, we're talking."

"Hmm. Keep me posted. 'Bye. Gotta go. They're recapping the golf tournament from this weekend. I'll tell your mom you said, "'Bye". Love you."

"Okay, Daddy," she said to the empty phone line. Her daddy had hung up on her! When he was done talking, he was done. They had adjusted to such abrupt endings to phone conversations.

She was finished with dinner when her cell phone rang. It was her girlfriend Karen. Toni and Karen had met at an outdoor concert one summer in Balboa Park and immediately hit it off. Since then, they talked at least twice per week. Meeting for dinner was not always possible, since Karen was a Border Patrol agent and worked a shift that changed every few months. Due to all the changes since 9/11, she also worked a good amount of overtime.

"Hello, Carina! Long time, no hear from you!" Toni told her friend, calling her by a Spanish play on her name, "Carina", that meant "dear".

"Well, you know. Work is busy, and well, my husband keeps me busy, too," Karen laughingly replied. Karen had married the love of her life shortly before she met Toni. Karen and her husband Allan lived in one of the many suburbs of Chula Vista, which was south of San Diego.

"Oh, please! Girl, if you and Allan actually see the rest of your house, it's a miracle. From the bedroom to the bathroom and back to the bedroom. Five bedrooms and you use only one. *"No time to eat! We's got lovin' to do!"*"

Allan was from South Carolina, so he and Toni got along just fine as fellow Southerners. She often teased the retired Navy officer about his drawl which, while considerably less noticeable than when he entered the military full-time as a young lieutenant out of college over twenty years ago, could still be heard. Allan was ten years older than Karen at forty-seven. While Karen didn't tell tales, contrary to her and Toni's constant teasing, Allan apparently had energy to spare after dedicating his life to the country and starting his own electrical engineering firm. Her friend kept a smile on her face.

"Hater!" Karen laughed again.

"I'm with you when you're right," Toni laughed right back.

"Allan says to tell you hi. I'm on a day shift now, so he's quite happy as you can imagine."

"Give him a hug for me. Tell him I'm still waiting on my sweet potato pie." She heard a side conversation between Karen and Allan.

"He says he will have one for you this weekend, but you have to come and get it."

"I'm there already. I'll see you on Saturday."

"So, Toni, what's been going on? Any news on the guy you got caught checking out?"

"Well, we went to lunch today. He's supposed to call this evening."

"You went to lunch? Business or pleasure?" she asked Toni rather silkily.

"Business, of course. You know me," Toni replied. "Except it ended up being pleasure, and somehow I ended up agreeing to see if things will work outside of the office."

"Baaaack up! You, Miss Strictly Chocolate, decided that you would date a white man and one who's a client at that?"

"I know. Crazy, isn't it? Karen, he moves me. I can't explain why I said yes, but I knew that I couldn't say no. As much as I wanted to—my head certainly said no. You know how I am about office romances. If they can go wrong, they will. He's different. Could turn out that he's different "bad", but I don't know. I had a weird dream last night—"

Toni stopped because her phone beeped signaling another call. She looked at the phone display and saw that it was a local number she didn't recognize. Although Gabe had given her his card when she went to APEX for her proposal, she had been busy and did not have a chance to look at the numbers.

"I think this is him, Karen. I will let him go to voicemail."

"Oh, no, you won't. Bye! Call me!" Karen hung up the telephone allowing Toni time to answer the other call.

"This is Toni Quinn."

"Toni, this is Gabe. How are you this evening?"

"I'm fine. How are you?"

"Tired. It was a busy day. I couldn't stop thinking about you, though."

"Umm, you don't waste time. Does "build up to the moment" mean anything to you?"

"It used to. Believe it or not, I'm a fairly reserved person, but with you I just let go. Wonder why?"

"I'm not even going to try and answer that. I can only come out on the other side as shallow or shallower," Toni laughed her response.

"Hmm. I'm into deep things myself," he teased.

"Okay. You're scaring me! I asked if we could take this slow."

"I remember. I replied that you could ask, but that *I* wouldn't make any guarantees. I decided that I needed to be fast on the take with you."

"Why is that?"

"Sooner or later the men in San Diego will figure out what a gem you are, and I'll be left out in the cold for having moved too slow."

"Well…my head is getting larger and larger the longer this conversation continues. If it's any consolation, now that I've accepted this—this *thing*—between us, I don't feel like moving slowly, but slow is probably the better route. I feel like things have completely flipped upside down."

"Hmm," Gabe replied.

A companionable silence existed for a few moments, with each gathering his or her thoughts on the matter at hand. How slow to go was the question when all each really wanted to do was explore the sensation, the fire that existed between the two of them. Neither had ever known such chemistry with any other person.

"Toni?"

"Yes, Gabe," Toni answered in a voice that sounded way too familiar and way, way too natural to her own ears.

I've only just met the man, and I sound like I've known him forever. Granted, he's kissed me like I was a cold glass of lemonade on a hot Florida day. Just thinking of the kiss gave Toni's body a taste of lunchtime pleasure. *Calm down, Toni, just take it easy.*

"I'm going to be busy tomorrow preparing for this week's travel. Before I go, though, I want to tell you something."

"You're not married, are you?"

"Where did that come from? Never mind. No, I'm not married and have never been married. What about you?"

"No, I've never been married, Gabe."

"Okay. That's out of the way. Back to what I was say-ing— "

"Yes?"

"I'm going to be busy, but I'm going to come see you before I leave tomorrow."

"Okay."

"Well, I'm going to take you for a ride, if you'll allow me to. I'll call and see what time is good."

"Fine," she replied, wondering what he was up to.

"Good night. See you tomorrow."

"Good night, Gabe. See you."

As she clicked off her cell phone, Toni pondered the sudden, if unexpected, action in her social life. *Hmm. What's in the air at that coffee shop?!*

The next work day went smoothly. Toni stayed in a state of anticipation. She smiled, worked hard, and thought hard about how her logical life seemed to be shaping into something completely illogical by her standards. Twists and turns that were completely unanticipated had her pondering what else could happen.

Gabe called around six-thirty, at the end of her working day. Toni typically worked late, something she had advised the APEX executives of when they were considering her firm. Her day often ended with her wrapping up things that were pushed to the back burner while she consulted with client personnel. This was fine with her. It was often quiet at client sites this time of evening. APEX still had a number of folks around.

"Hey," Gabe said after she answered the office telephone.

"Hey yourself," she replied.

"Can you take a break right now?"

"Certainly. I'm wrapping things up. Can you give me a few minutes so that I can completely shut down?"

"Hmm mmm. Go ahead. I'm almost finished here. Meet me at reception, will you, please?"

"No problem. See you in a few."

Both worked the last few minutes with anticipation building. After meeting at reception, Gabe reached for Toni's hand with his, only to retract it after she gave him a look that would have done in a lesser man. *Ouch! That must have been what Sam was talking about. That look would have cut if I didn't know she was concerned about work.*

After reaching the garage, Gabe asked Toni about the floor on which she had parked.

"I'm on three."

"So am I. Let's go."

"Where are we going?"

"To your car."

"No, *where* are we going? You said you were going to take me for a ride."

"Can't wait, huh? Just a few more minutes."

"Gabe, you should know that I don't do surprises," she told him in a very serious tone.

"I'll keep that in mind," he replied in a tone that was just as unserious as hers was serious.

"Right!"

"Which is your car?"

"The navy 5-series over there," she told him.

"Nice wheels."

"Thanks."

He loaded her roller bag into her trunk.

"Hmm. We're going a short distance. It may be better if you follow me instead of our having to come back here to retrieve your car."

"Again, where *are* we going?"

"Patience," he told her.

Both got into their cars and started them. Gabe pulled out, and Toni fell in behind him. After a few minutes of driving, they reached a parking lot near one of the beaches. The waters around SoCal were rather cool this time of year, so not many people were out, except some die-hard surfers. Gabe got out, walked over to Toni's car, and opened her door. She looked up at him, with an eyebrow raised.

"The beach?" she asked.

"Yes, the beach," he told her as she quickly removed the trouser socks and loafers she had on to avoid a sand invasion. She noticed that Gabriel had removed his shoes. *He must have done that while driving.* She had noticed him leaning down a couple of times, but since the SUV had not swerved, she'd assumed that he had dropped something. He waited until she finished. *Nice feet,* he thought, as he got his first look at them unshod.

Gabe reached for her key, closed her door, and zapped the remote for the lock.

"First things first," he said.

"What—" Toni started, only to find herself back up against the driver side of the BMW with Gabe's mouth making a fast descent while his hands took the hairpins out of her bun, which was a natural style that day.

"I've waited all day," he whispered as he nipped at her lips while massaging her scalp. "I missed you today."

"Oh, did you?" Toni whispered back in a saucy voice.

"Oh, I did. Certainly, at that." He nipped at her lips again, teasing her, adding kindling to the fire that was already simmering between the two of them.

"Gabe?" Toni called softly.

"Hmm?" he answered in a voice as soft.

"If you're going to kiss me, please go ahead and do so. *I've* been waiting all day, too."

"My pleasure," as he opened his mouth against hers to release some of the day's anticipation. *What is it about this woman?* he asked himself as he tenderly explored her mouth, increasing the pressure against Toni's lips.

This man can kiss! These lips ought to be illegal, she thought, as she looped her arms around his neck. His body came a bit closer as she applied a bit of pressure, but not as close as she desired. So, she moved her arms from around his neck and put them around his waist, silently telling him that she wanted him close.

Gabe received her message loud and clear, but was not going to comply. He was already struggling, and if he leaned against her, any and all modesty would be gone. He came just a bit closer, offering her some of what she wanted.

"Gabe?" Toni said as she turned her head to the side.

"Hmm mmm?" he replied as he rested his chin on her head and arms on the top of the car.

"What's wrong?"

"Nothing's wrong."

"You're kissing me, but—"

"But what?" knowing what she was going to say.

"But you aren't really touching me."

"There's a reason for that."

"What reason?"

"Toni, I'm trying to keep a little modesty going here."

"Forget modesty. If you're going to kiss me, kiss me," she told him firmly.

Gabe looked around, not really caring whether people noticed him and Toni. His concern was for her. He was so hungry for her touch, to feel her body next to his that he thought he would faint if his body came into full contact with hers. He could not resist. This woman, this hold she had on him, this web he was in could not be explained. He decided to give her what she asked for without restraint.

"Toni," Gabe whispered her name while gently turning her head back towards him.

"Yes?"

"I'm going to kiss you," he told her with his green eyes so dark they were almost black from tamped down passion.

"Really?" she smiled.

"Yes. And I'm going to touch you," he gently told her while putting his hands back in her hair.

"Really?" she asked as she again looped her arms around his neck.

"Really," as his mouth lowered toward hers and his body came flush against hers.

He placed his lips against hers again, nipping a couple of times to open her mouth. She willingly did so, and he swept in. He kissed her with a passion that transcended anything either of them had ever felt. Their tongues tangled, and their bodies meshed. The essence of one called to the essence of the other. Gabe's hands left Toni's hair to travel down her back, down her sides, and to finally grasp her hips. Their bodies seemed to fuse together, and Toni gave a gasp when she felt how hard he was against her and just how wonderful it felt to have his body leaning into hers.

Gabe thought that he really *would* expire from the pleasure of having Toni in his arms. This was more than he could have imagined. She felt right at home in his arms. It was as if his arms had been waiting for this perfect fit, for this very woman, who was not what he expected, but was who he suspected he needed. He gave her everything he could in the kiss, in the pressure of his body against hers. He needed air. He eased up. Toni gulped in some air, looked up at him with both passion and fear warring on her eyes.

"Gabe?" she gasped.

Not giving her a chance to think, he started kissing her all over again. He switched their positions so that he was against the car and she leaned into him. *Oh, that was the wrong move,* he thought. He was lost. Toni took her position of power and wielded it like a medieval sword. She kissed him like it was the last time. She subtly rubbed her chest against his causing him to moan like he was in pain. She was merciless in her pursuit as her tongue swept inside his mouth, dueling in passion.

Finally, the two of them realized they were at the brink of truly becoming arrest material for San Diego County's finest. They eased apart, breathing hard like thoroughbreds that had run the race of their lives. Gabe kept his arms around Toni's hips and held her close. He loved having her in his arms, but she served as a shield for the passionate expression his body was making at that moment. Although there were fewer people around than when they first arrived, he did not want to put Toni at risk or embarrass her in any way.

When their breathing had slowed considerably after several minutes of just calming down against each other,

Gabe reached for Toni's chin where her head rested on his shoulder. Her eyes were closed, although her head was up.

"Look at me."

Her eyes slowly opened. The chocolate orbs were as black and slumberous with passion as his green ones.

"Toni."

"Hmm," she moaned, licking her lips with a quick swipe of her tongue.

"Toni. Don't."

"Hmm," she moaned again.

Gabe could only do what was clearly becoming natural with her. He leaned down and kissed her again. Her eyes open; his eyes open. Each saw the fierce passion resting in the other, knowing that when the passion was fully realized, there was no guarantee that either would survive the burn.

Once again, they stopped and rested against each other.

"I have dinner," he whispered.

"You do?"

"Yes. It's in the truck. If we move, we may be able to catch the sunset."

"Okay," she said without moving.

"Toni."

"Hmm."

"Sweetheart, you have to move so that I can move," he told her while gently moving her so that she could rest against the car.

He opened the passenger door of his truck and pulled out the hamper a local company had delivered to him earlier in the afternoon. As he turned around and stopped, he was painfully aware that she could see that his body had not recovered from their passionate embraces. A flush settled on his cheeks as Toni looked at his body squarely where his pants were tented with the evidence of his arousal. Her eyes studied his body as if she had x-ray vision. This did not help him at all. They traveled up his body, looking at his waist, lingering on his chest, noting the shape of his shoulders, the strong neck muscles, skimming his lips, to land on his eyes. She looked at him and in him without saying a word.

Then she very softly told him, "You scare me, Gabe. But I think I am more scared of not knowing where such emotion, such passion could lead. I have never experienced this before, so I'm asking that you please be patient with me. As free as this passion with you comes, fear attacks me at the same time."

"I know. I promise to try to take it easy. I don't want to hurt you, but neither do I want to get hurt. I'm thirty-nine years old, and this has never happened to me. Fear comes at me, too, but there is this assurance that I would be missing out on a life changing experience if I did not get to know you, pursue this, and pursue you. So, fair warning. We'll slow down a bit, while we're still moving forward. Fair enough?"

"Fair enough."

"Let's catch the sunset and have some dinner." He grabbed her hand so that they could walk the short distance to the sandy shore.

They watched the sun settle over the Pacific Ocean while having a dinner of cold chicken salad, roasted vegetables, cheeses, fruits, desserts and wine. The dinner was very good, but each understood that the company was much more enjoyable. Each pondered what the future held in store for them, even while they laughed, teased, shared things about themselves, and generally thought how they would miss each other while he was on travel.

Gabe sensed that Toni was vulnerable—not fragile—but vulnerable after what had happened. He could not tell her what he knew, what had become amazingly clear to him during their time together that evening. She would become his wife. There was so much more to find out about her, but before the year was out, she would be Mrs. Gabriel Jackson. *Okay, maybe she would be Mrs. Antoinette Quinn-Jackson.* He could live with that, he thought, as he gave her a kiss on the cheek as the sun disappeared.

Chapter 7

"Gabe, we're having dinner next Thursday, and I'd like you to come. It's been a few weeks since we've seen you, so I expect you to be here. Your sisters and their husbands will be here, as well. Are you planning to bring a date?" his mother, Ellen, asked.

"I don't know, Mom. Why? I'm not enough all by myself?" he teased his mother. As the middle child and only son, Gabe had a particularly close relationship with his mother. Ellen respected her son as an adult, but that did not keep her from throwing hints his way when she had opportunity.

"Son, you're plenty by yourself; however, I'm only asking so that I can prepare accordingly. In any case, let me know by Tuesday of next week, okay?"

"Sure thing. Thursday should be great, as I plan to go to Chicago the following week. Put Dad on the line, will you?"

After a few minutes of talking with his dad, Gabe returned the phone to its base. He went to his workshop—he loved carpentry—to continue working on the cradle he was crafting for his youngest sister, Allison, who was pregnant with his parents' first grandchild. They were all quite excited, including his older sister, Marian, who had yet to have children. The handmade cradle would be a masterpiece for the welcome addition to their family.

His mother's question was on his mind. *Should I invite Toni?* Meeting his family this early might scare her away. While he was harmless, he was very sure about Toni. He did not understand why. All he knew was that Toni had captured him from the beginning. This was something to think about.

Pulling a green shirt from the closet, and a pair of black pants, Gabe got ready for work on Monday morning. While his trip was successful, he was looking forward to getting back in the office. Gabe did not practice lying to himself. *You just want to see, Toni,* he told himself. Gabe had called Toni each evening while he was away on travel. There was no need to pretend that he was calling her for any other reason than to get to know her. He asked about her family and told her about his. Surprisingly, they both had a couple of siblings each. While he was sandwiched in the middle, Toni was the oldest in her crew. This likely explained her frank and aggressive nature. Running her own company probably meant that she had to be that way. He was fully aware of how women could be treated in business.

He was excited to see her. Over the weekend while working on his sister's cradle, he thought about the type of cradle he would make for his own children if he were so blessed. He wondered if Toni wanted children. She had told him that she was almost thirty-six, which made her three years younger than his thirty-nine. Not too old in his opinion for children, but that would be something they would need to discuss since pregnancies could potentially be a bit more difficult the older a woman became.

Once at the office, Gabe got straight to work. He needed to talk to Sam about the Chicago office. They had already planned to have Toni go there as part of her contracted work, but after speaking with the personnel there, she may need to go sooner. He would need to figure out if she could rearrange the schedule she had provided them. The bulk of the test team was located in Chicago, and some help was needed there.

"Rachel, I'm going to Sam's office. I will likely be gone for the rest of the hour at least," he told his assistant while walking out of his suite of offices to go up to Sam's office.

"Gabe, don't forget that you have a staff meeting this afternoon," Rachel responded.

"I know. See if you can move it to three o'clock instead of two. I know that there is a requirements review with Vista Medical, and a few of the team members will be in that session. On second thought, cancel today's staff meeting and reschedule for Wednesday, please."

"Okay. If you need me to bring you anything while you're meeting with Sam, give me a ring."

"Thanks, Rachel. You're the best."

"I hear you."

Gabe took the stairs one floor up to the main floor which was the 15th. APEX occupied four floors in the building. Sam wanted to keep his office on the main floor to ensure that visiting clients did not have to go up and down elevators in order to meet with him when necessary. There was plenty of conference space on the floor, so this made it easy to conduct business.

Sam looked up from his desk when he heard Gabe greeting Shawna. Shawna was Sam's executive assistant; she was also his cousin. At twenty-seven she was one of the youngest out of his first cousins, but she was also highly organized. He was quite fortunate to have her working with him. She kept him on task and as his cousin, she kept an eye on those women who would try to cross the line with him.

As a practice, unless it was something that was confidential, she sat in on meetings with female personnel. If she could not, then Sam usually left his door open. He loved Denni and was not willing to let anyone come between that love. It was not worth the headache.

"Morning, Gabe," Sam got up and gave him their typical man-hug.

"Morning, Sam," Gabe responded.

"How was Chicago?"

"It was productive, but I am thinking that we may need to get Toni to go to Chicago sooner than planned. I was there for one of the test cycles for the customizations we did for Valley Medical, and it was ugly, Sam. They had to stop a couple of times to call in the business analyst who did the requirements. While she had not done the test cases—the test analyst had—there was apparently a real disconnect. We have a bit of time for this release because the project manager was wise enough to build in some extra time, but if this is the way each test cycle has gone, no wonder we are having sketchy releases."

"Well, this is your area. Do what you think is necessary. Will you go back this week to help with the Valley Medical issues?"

"No, I don't think so. Last week, I had Rachel set up a daily call with the team so that I can get updates. I've got the managers and their teams on conference for a half-hour every day. I do think that we should get Toni booked for next week, though. She will have to rearrange the schedule that she provided us, but this release is important. The rollout for Valley will be for six locations, but if the first one fails, then that is going to leave them with a bad impression."

"I agree. It is good that we have grown so quickly, but the growth has not been without its share of problems, Gabe.

I want the Valley rollout to go well, just as you do, so get Toni booked. You're going with her, I take it?"

"Absolutely."

They spent a couple more hours discussing other projects. They were very busy, and they needed to catch up since Gabe had been out of town. Their session yielded what they already knew: Toni was going to be a huge help if she could get their development activities turned around. They were thinking of expanding to an app for customers, but with the current state of things, it would be a waste of time and money—and very premature.

"Speaking of Toni, how are things going with that project?"

"Going well. Mom invited me for dinner on Thursday with the rest of the family. I am thinking about asking her to go with me."

"You're asking her to go to meet the family?"

"I *am thinking* about it."

"You don't think it's kind of early?"

"I do, and I don't. I talked with her every evening while I was away, although not Saturday and Sunday. I am sure about her, Sam. Better for her to meet them now."

Sam sighed. "I don't know, Gabe. You know how folks can be. It is one thing to have me for a friend, and we know how long it took for your family to warm to me. It's another for you to marry someone black. I don't want either of you to get hurt. You already know that you're a brother to me, and I want you to be happy."

"I'm not fooling myself. It will be a surprise for them if she came with me. I would rather find out early where things stand. I'm not changing where she is concerned and better for them to know that upfront."

"Okay, Man. Your call. Have you asked her?"

"No, I need to meet with her today about Chicago, so I plan to ask her then."

"More power to you."

"Thanks, Man. You know I'm going to need it."

"Tell Toni hi for me."

72

Chapter 8

"Rachel, can you get Toni on the phone, please? I need to meet with her as soon as possible. See if she's free at 1PM," Gabe asked as he walked back into his office suite.

"Sure thing."

Rachel called Toni as instructed.

"Toni, good morning. This is Rachel, Gabe's assistant. He would like to meet with you at 1PM today. Do you have time?"

"I need to rearrange a session, but I can be there," Toni responded.

"Okay. I'll let him know," concluding the call.

She pressed the intercom button to speak with Gabe.

"Gabe, she'll be over at one o'clock."

"Thanks, Rachel. We'll probably be busy for an hour or so."

"All right."

Toni checked her lip gloss in her mirror before she got ready to walk over to Gabe's office. Although they had spoken while he was out of town, they did not speak over the weekend. Some friends from Seattle visited over the weekend to help celebrate her birthday with her local crew, and she had told him that she would not be available. She was *really* feeling this man. She needed a breather to make sure her head was on straight. She had never felt or thought this way about a man in a very long time, and she needed to be sure it wasn't just something due to her having not dated in quite some time and frankly, because he got her body humming.

Well, here we go, she told herself as she locked up her handbag in the desk drawer and left her office.

"Hi. I am here to see Gabe. I'm Toni Quinn, the consultant."

"Hi! I'm Rachel Parks. We talked on the phone, but it is very nice to put a face with the voice. I am sorry that I could not meet you before now," Rachel told her.

"No problem, and likewise, Rachel."

"I'll get Gabe for you. He is on the telephone at the moment. Please have a seat."

Rachel opened Gabe's door and mouthed to him that Toni had arrived. Gabe acknowledged her with a nod and three fingers to let her know that he needed a bit of time.

"Gabe is wrapping up the call. May I get you a bottle of water while you wait?"

"Yes, thank you."

As Toni sipped her water, she thought about the last time she saw Gabe. The beach picnic. *Lord, that man is some kind of fine. Stay focused. This is work.* After several minutes, she heard Gabe's door open, and there he was. *It ought to be a sin for a man to look this good. That green shirt is a perfect match for his eyes. I'm done. Just done.*

"Toni, good afternoon. Come on in. Rachel, will you hold my calls, please, unless it is an emergency."

"Yes, I will. Let me know if you need anything."

Toni walked towards Gabe with her legs trembling. *Fiddlesticks! Get it together, Girl!* Gabe smiled at her, and all she could think about was their last kiss. Gabe held out his hand and she shook it, turning her head towards the view beyond his window, while he pushed the door closed with his other hand.

"Toni," Gabe said huskily.

"Hi, Gabe," she said, not looking at him.

"Toni, before we get started. I need to tell you something. I missed you."

"Oh. I missed you, too," she responded in a whisper.

"Toni. Look at me."

Toni turned her head towards him.

"I know we're at work, but I needed to tell you that."

"Umm, okay…"

Gabe turned Toni around to face him, and put his hands underneath her cheeks and lowered his head. Toni could not resist, so she met him halfway. Gabe teased her lips, nipping at them until she opened them. His tongue swept inside so that he could reach every crevice and convey to her how much he missed her. Toni met him in his quest. Her tongue wrestled with his so that she could show him how much *she* missed him. Totally out of character for her in the workplace, she simply could not make herself not yield to the passion that sizzled between them. This man floated her boat unlike any other. She caressed his scalp as they allowed the passion to sweep over them. Finally, they needed to take a breath. Gabe pulled Toni to his chest and allowed her to rest against him. After a few minutes, they were able to step back and look at each other.

"This is real for me, Toni. I have never dated someone that I worked closely with—never."

"Well, I don't go around kissing clients, either, you know," Toni responded.

"I know. You are the consummate professional. I think that this—between us—is stronger than our work boundaries. I do not want to make you uncomfortable, but I do not want to miss this."

"Okay. So, this is slowing down a bit, huh?" she teased. "Gabe, can you do dinner tonight?"

"I was going to ask you. I should be free here around six-thirty. Will you be around?"

"Yes. We can leave from here."

"I'll drive. I can follow you home. That will keep you from having to drive from here."

"Okay."

Gabe gave her another short kiss, then walked her over to the small conference table in his office. He snagged his tablet from his desk and proceeded to go over the results of his trip to Chicago.

He explained the problems and what they were facing, being clear about what he thought about the operation, while stressing the importance of the first release for Valley Medical.

"So, I think it would be helpful if you made a trip to Chicago next week. I know that this is earlier than your plan, but this is a critical release for us."

"Okay. Will someone from here be going, as well?"

"I will be going with you."

"Oh!"

"Yes, oh. I think it will be better for me to be there to help with resolution and quick implementation. I would like to be there first thing Monday morning. Are you available to fly out on Sunday?"

"Yes, I can fly on Sunday."

"Let me get Rachel so that she can make the arrangements. We usually stay at Marriott properties. Will that work for you?"

"Yes, that is fine."

Gabe got up and walked to the door. Sticking his head outside, he saw that Rachel was not on the telephone.

"Rachel, can you come in for a sec?"

"Yes."

Rachel came in and sat where Gabe indicated at the conference table. A great assistant, Rachel had her pad and pencil ready. Gabe explained what was needed, ensuring to tell her to reserve conference space at the offices in Chicago, with some extra monitors for Toni's use. Gabe had an office there, but he didn't think it was wise to have Toni with him in his office. He didn't think he would be able to keep his hands off of her. *Man, this woman has got me going.*

"I'll send you both the information once I have everything settled," Rachel told them. "Do you need rental cars or do you want car service?"

"One rental car should be fine. Toni?" Gabe asked.

"I'm fine with that. Thank you."

"Okay. I'll get right on this," Rachel said, rising from her chair.

"Thank you. You're the best."

"You're welcome. I know," she told Gabe.

Gabe looked at Toni. "Thank you for being so accommodating. I really appreciate it."

"No problem. By the way, Rachel was very helpful and efficient with arranging things for me for the initial proposal. I need to get back for my afternoon sessions. Anything else?"

"No. I'll see you at six-thirty. I'm looking forward to it."

"So am I." Toni walked out of Gabe's office, knowing full well that he watched her butt this time. She gave him a little extra something to look at since he was looking. *Sweat that out, Gabe.*

Chapter 9

Toni and Gabe both made the best of the afternoon at work, but their kiss was at the forefront of both their minds. The passion was real. "100" in the words of the young folks. Neither had experienced anything like this in their past relationships. This was brand new territory, and frankly, it was a bit daunting.

Toni shut down her computer and gathered her things for the evening. Gabe had done the same thing and met her at the elevator. They rode down in silence. The tension was so thick that neither of them trusted themselves to say anything.

Gabe walked Toni to her vehicle.

"I'll follow you home, okay?"

"Okay. I'm not too far from here. Maybe a half hour this time of evening."

"Okay."

Toni backed out of her space and made her way to the garage gate. She could see Gabe in her rearview mirror. Leela James's "Fall For You" came on through her stereo. The irony was not lost on her. She engaged her Bluetooth system to call her sister.

When her sister answered, Toni told her, "Reece, I'm in trouble."

Gabe pulled out of the garage. He engaged his Bluetooth and called Sam.

When Sam answered, Gabe told him, "Sam, I'm in trouble."

Toni opened the garage and pulled her car inside. Taking her stuff out of the car, she gestured to Gabe to get out and come in for a second. Gabe turned off his car and entered the house with her through the garage door.

"Couple minutes while I put this away. Have a seat, please," Toni told him.

"No rush."

Toni went to her office, reflecting on her conversation with Reecie. Reecie had responded to Toni's opening comment with, "What's wrong?"

"I'm falling for this guy, Reecie. Fast. I don't know what to do." She recounted what had occurred in the office earlier that day.

"Well, Toni, could it be that Gabe is the man you have been waiting for?"

"Quite possibly, Reecie. He told me that he was serious."

"Believe the man, then."

"Easier said than done. He's white, and this is so fast!"

"Who said love would come like one of your plans? Look the way you expect? Maybe you need to relax and just see what happens."

"I guess," she sighed. "Thanks, Sis. Love you much."

"Love you, too. Bye."

While Toni was in her office, Gabe was looking at the pictures placed around the living room and thinking about his brief conversation with Sam.

"Toni, I take it?"

"Yeah, Man."

"You've been in trouble since you met her. That ain't new," Sam said with a smile in his voice. "Seriously, though. What's really going through your mind?"

"I don't want to scare her away, Sam. This woman is the real deal. I don't want to get this wrong."

"Go easy, Gabe. Give her time to catch up with you."

"Yeah. Hard when I just want to…"

"I know. Remember? You were there when I met Denni. I understand, but you also remember how I almost lost her because I was rushing, not making what she thought a priority? Avoid that, my friend. If she's the one, then she's worth you slowing down a bit."

"I get it. Thanks, Bro."

"Anytime."

Gabe resolved to slow down. Toni was definitely worth it.

Toni took a deep breath before leaving her office. *Lord, please let me make it through this date. Don't let me jump this man's bones.* She smiled. She was feeling some kind of sexy this evening. *The attention of a good man will do that, Girl!*

"Gabe, I'm ready. Thanks for waiting."

"No problem. I saw your pictures. Your parents and siblings?"

"Yes. My parents live in Florida as I told you before."

She picked up a picture. "This is me with Reece—we also call her Reecie—and Alex."

In their conversations, she had not told him the professions of her sister and brother, so she wasn't surprised when Gabe asked, "Isn't that Alexander Quinn from the NBA?"

"Yes, he's my little brother."

"When you told me about his name on the telephone, I didn't make the connection. I take it that you do not see your siblings much since they are both on the opposite side of the country?"

"This is true. We try to make it to a couple of Alex's games throughout the year so that we can be together. He gets a bit more time during the off-season, but not much since he's training during that time, as well."

They walked to Gabe's car. Always the gentleman, Gabe opened her door for her.

Gabe backed his SUV out of the driveway and then took Toni's hand in his. Neither said a word. It was a comfortable silence, but it was a passion-packed one, as well. The current moving between them from simply holding hands had both of them subtly shifting in their seats. A Sir Charles Jones song came on the radio, "For Your Love". Gabe turned to Toni. His eyes said it all, and Toni understood what they were saying. He would go the distance for this passion they were both experiencing.

They arrived at Fashion Valley Mall in Mission Valley. A popular outdoor mall, the area was busy at all times of the day since it boasted premier shops and eateries.

Gabe pulled into the parking garage and turned to look at Toni. Toni looked at him and then leaned over the console. No words were needed.

The kiss consumed them. Like a match to dry paper, their lips fused with such fire that both felt like they were burning up.

"Gabe..." Toni breathed.

"Toni. Babe, I..."

"Don't stop."

Gabe pulled Toni closer to him and kissed her like there was no one around. The taste of her was sweet. He was all in.

Toni kissed him back with equal fervor. *Fiddlesticks! I'm done. So, so done!*

Gabe eased from the kiss. "Toni…"

"I know. Let's go eat. We really need to stop with the parking lots," she teased to help ease the tension and lighten the mood.

"I know, right?"

Dinner was easy, as they enjoyed the food at an upscale Italian eatery. They talked, savoring the opportunity to find out more about the other. They found out that they had a few more things in common, and found out that they were opposites in some other ways, too.

Gabe asked Toni about dinner with his family.

"My family is having dinner on Thursday. I would like you to join me. Will you?"

"Your family?"

"Yes, my family. My parents and sisters with their husbands. Toni, you know how I feel about you. Because of that, I think you should meet my family."

"Umm…okay. I was not expecting to meet your family. At least, not this early," she responded.

"It won't be bad."

"Do they know I'm black?"

"No, I have not told them that I'm dating you. Are you asking if I think it will be a problem? No, I don't, but I think it will be a surprise to them, since I have never dated anyone black."

"Hmm. Well, if we're going to do this, then I guess it's better now than later. Oh, all right. I'll go," Toni replied slowly.

"Well, don't be so eager."

"It's not that, Gabe. Families can be fine with friends from different cultures, but think something totally different when a child or sibling starts dating someone who doesn't have the same background or who doesn't look the same. We're grown folk, but we still have families. I will tell you that my parents will raise their eyebrows, ask me if my head is on straight, and we'll move on. I am not asking you to tell me how your family will react, but you should be honest first with yourself. I'll go. I'm going because of how *I* feel and what *I* think about you. For the record."

"Okay."

"Certainly."

They concluded dinner with a lovely key lime dessert that reminded Toni of home.

"Let's go. We have a busy rest of the week," Gabe told Toni as he signed the dinner receipt.

"Yes. Things are going well, but there are a number of recommendations I am going to make," said Toni as they walked back to Gabe's vehicle, holding hands.

As they passed a group of white women, one of them rolled her eyes at them. Toni looked at Gabe to see if he'd caught the disrespectful gesture.

"That's the kind of foolishness I'm talking about, Gabe."

"I saw her, and I'm ignoring her. I'm with you. Now, back to *our* conversation regarding work. I expect that you will have a number of recommendations."

"I don't want things to be a big surprise."

"Well, we knew what we were hiring you to do, so no real surprise in that you are going to make recommendations."

"Hmm. What time is dinner on Thursday, Gabe?"

"Dinner is at 7. With traffic, it is hard to get us all there before then. I'll pick you up from your house, okay?"

"That's fine. I'll leave a little early from work since I will want to freshen up."

"Toni?"

"Yes?"

"Thank you."

Gabe pulled up to Toni's house, which was a renovated craftsman style house with a porch. The house was sage in color with white trim. It was very inviting and deceivingly spacious on the inside.

Walking her to the front door, Gabe held her hand. Toni leaned into his side. She loved the feel of the strength of his body. He was tall and fit with defined muscles, and she loved the solid feel of him. He felt like he could handle things. She wasn't fooling herself about the relationship. He was white, and she was black. That alone was plenty. Every relationship got tested. She believed that he could pass the tests that would come their way. He was mentally stable—no crazy stuff had come across in their interactions. In past encounters with other men, she had heard some wild stuff; Gabe was not that way.

"Would you like to come in for a few minutes?"

"I think I better go home. I've a couple of early calls in the morning."

"Okay."

Toni wrapped her arms around his neck, pulled his head down, and laid a kiss on him that had him breathing hard in no time. *This woman.*

He wrapped his arms around her waist, slid his hands to the curve of her butt, and brought her in close. He angled his head for better access; Toni accommodated him. The kiss represented all they were experiencing—the connection, the passion, and the thrill of new love.

"Gabe," Toni sighed.

"Yeah, babe?" Gabe whispered as he nibbled on her lips, easing them, once again, out of a consuming kiss.

"I think I better go inside now."

"Uh huh," as he continued to nibble.

Toni nipped his lips. "Seriously. Any more and things will go farther than I think either of us is ready for—well, besides our bodies, that is."

Gabe sighed. "You're right. I want more than your body, Toni. I'm in for the long haul, so…"

"Okay. Good night, Gabe."

"Good night, Toni."

Gabe kissed her lightly one last time. He waited until she opened her door and he heard the lock click from the inside. *Another cold shower,* he thought.

Chapter 10

Thursday dawned with Gabe and Toni both thinking about the dinner with his family that they were attending that evening. Gabe did not know how his family would respond, but he knew their surprise was a sure bet. Toni had no idea what to expect.

Both worked throughout the day, with Gabe calling Toni shortly before five o'clock to let her know that he was leaving and that he would pick her up around six-thirty. Toni told him that she would be ready.

At home, Toni walked into her generously filled closet to find something to wear. After looking at a few dresses, she finally settled on a royal blue dress. Blue was her favorite color, and she found that she felt more confident when she wore some shade of it, especially, when there was temptation to be nervous. Meeting Gabe's family required some assurance.

Gabe was there at six-thirty. He walked her to the car.

"Is there anything you would like to listen to?"

"No, this is fine. By the way, why are you always playing R&B when I get in your vehicle?"

Gabe laughed. "What? 'Cause I'm white I can't listen to R&B?"

Toni laughed, as well. "No, that's not what I'm saying. Well, not really. I just wondered why!"

"Well, Sam and I were roommates in college. He intro-duced me to R&B. I've been hooked ever since. I still listen to other music, but I find that there is a song for every mood with R&B and soul music."

"Yeah, that's true."

They pulled up to Gabe's parents' home which was a modern stone home with a long porch for the length of the front of the house. Perched where it was, one could see some of the Pacific Ocean.

"Beautiful home. The view from the back must be awesome," Toni told him.

"It is. They built this shortly before they retired. They said that they were not building another home, so they built this one the way they wanted."

"Makes sense to me. It is lovely."

Gabe held her hand as they walked up the steps. It looked as if his sister and their husbands were already there, as other cars were in the circular driveway.

"Ready? You okay?" he asked.

"Yep. Let's do this."

Gabe rang the doorbell in lieu of using his key. His dad, Stephen, answered the door.

"Hey, Son! Come on in."

"Hi, Dad! This is my lady friend, Toni. Toni, this is my dad, Stephen."

"Welcome, Toni. We're glad to have you."

"It is a pleasure to meet you, as well, Mr. Jackson."

"Please, call me Stephen. We're rather informal around here."

Stephen shook Toni's hand and walked them into the family room which was at the rear of the house, allowing them to enjoy the sweeping views on that side.

Gabe's sisters were at the big kitchen island talking with their mother. His sister, Allison was seated. Clearly, she was rather along in her pregnancy. Marian was standing, while their mother was putting the finishing touches on the dishes.

Gabe's brothers-in-law were seated in the family area, watching the game. Both looked up when Gabe and Toni walked in with Stephen.

"Everyone, this is Toni, Gabe's friend," announced Stephen.

Ellen looked up from a dish, and it was hard to miss the clear blink she gave upon seeing Toni. His sisters passed a look between them, and then to their husbands. Stephen seemed to be the only one who did not exhibit any visible shock at seeing Toni.

"Guys, this is Toni Quinn, my girlfriend. Toni, this is my mom, Ellen. My older sister, Marian Hall. My younger sister, Allison, who you can tell is very pregnant with my little niece. On the sofa is Brian, Marian's husband. In the chair is Patrick Ward, Allison's husband."

Toni walked over to Ellen, who was drying her hands on a dish towel so that she could shake Toni's hand.

"It's a pleasure to meet you, dear. Gabe called last night to tell us that he was bringing you, so we are quite glad to have you."

"Thank you, Mrs. Jackson. I am glad to be here this evening."

The rest of the crew came over to shake her hand and hug Gabe. The family was a group of huggers. For Toni, this was fine, since she was from a family of huggers, as well.

"You and Gabe have a seat. I'll be done in a few minutes. Stephen, will you get them something to drink, please, babe?" Ellen said.

Stephen fixed drinks. Everyone continued to chat as Ellen and Marian took the food to the dining room.

"We're ready," Marian announced.

Everyone sat down at the long table and reached out to the hand next to them. Toni raised an eyebrow. While she and Gabe blessed their food, she did not realize that it was because of a practice within his family.

Stephen said a short prayer, and everyone started passing dishes. From tender pot roast and scratch mashed potatoes, Ellen had cooked the things that her family enjoyed.

As Toni passed the asparagus dish accompanied by a white cream sauce, his sister Marian posed a question to her.

"So, Toni. I detect a bit of an accent. I take it that you are not from California?"

"No, Marian, I'm not. I am a native Floridian."

"Oh, where in Florida?"

"I am from the central part of the state. Northeast of Orlando."

"We have some friends who live in Ormond Beach. Are you close to there?"

"Yes, I am in the same county."

Ellen chimed in. "So, how did you and Gabe meet?"

Toni opened her mouth to answer, but Gabe responded instead.

"Toni's firm is providing us with some consulting services."

"Oh, you work together?" asked Patrick.

"Temporarily. Toni has her own firm, and we are one of her clients."

Brian and Patrick exchanged a look. Gabe saw the look and decided to address things head on. Toni was important to him, and his family needed to understand this. He rested his knife and fork, and grabbed Toni's hand under the table.

"Okay. It is clear that Toni and I have some visible differences. Toni and I encountered each other prior to her firm working with us. To my surprise, I saw her when I didn't think I had a chance of seeing her again."

"Where did you meet the first time?" asked Allison.

"A coffee shop, except I didn't know his name. I was a bit surprised to see him enter the conference room at APEX when I was there to give my pitch," answered Toni.

Stephen, understanding his son, decided to help Gabe out with his inquiry, so that he could get his family past this. At the end of the day, they all wanted Gabe to be happy.

"Gabe and Toni, while I am surprised to see the two of you together—for the obvious reason as I don't see any point to be shy about it—I hope you understand that I simply want you to be happy. Everyone will not see your relationship in the same way. Are you ready to deal with it?"

"Well, we have had some experiences. We get looks and have heard the odd comment, but we ignore them," Gabe answered. "We are both getting older, and the opinions of others matter less when we have both waited to meet the right partner."

"Ellen's parents didn't like me for a long time—pretty much until Marian came along. We are both white, so there are no guarantees either way."

Gabe's family expressed unreserved wishes for their success and continued a lively dinner in which they got to know Toni better and she them. They could see how much Gabe liked Toni. In return, they could see how much Toni liked him. Ellen caught Stephen's eye and subtly blew him a kiss when she did. Their son was happy, and that is what mattered.

Later that night, after their children had left, Ellen turned to Stephen while in bed.

"Stephen?"

"Yeah, babe?" wrapping his arm around her.

"Did it bother you that my parents didn't like you? I mean, *bother* you?"

"Yes and no. I was more concerned about you. I was determined to be with you even then, so I would have found a way, and I did. I gave you a baby," he laughed, kissing the top of her head while rubbing her forearm.

She tapped his shoulder, laughing along with him. "Yeah, Marian's birth changed things. Sad, though, that they missed enjoying you in the early years."

"Yes, but we recovered, dear."

"I'm happy for Gabe. He really likes her, and I can tell from the look in her eyes that she really likes him."

"Ellen, I think our son loves her. They are bound to have their tests. As I said earlier, there are no guarantees. You simply hope and believe for the best when it comes to love."

"Well, maybe we'll have a wedding before the year's out. Gabe's never been one to wait. He thinks and plans, but then he gets to doing what needs to be done."

"Maybe. Now, about babies. I don't want anymore—except grandchildren—but, I'm still very, very good at practicing," he teasingly told her, while pulling down the spaghetti strap of her gown and kissing her neck.

"Yes, you are...," Ellen whispered, as her body responded to his touch. She was amazed that after all this time and at the age of seventy for both of them, her husband was still able to make her breathless with just a touch and a look. She sincerely hoped that all her children had the same thing with their chosen mates. That was her last thought about her children for the rest of the night.

On the way home from dinner with his family, Gabe looked over at Toni. She was staring out the window, although she held his hand and squeezed it ever so often.

"So, what are you thinking, babe?" he asked.

"About dinner?" turning her head to look at him.

"Yes. My family, as well," he responded.

"Well, I think it is safe to say that they were surprised. I think it is also safe to say that their love for you meant that they got over their concerns rather quickly. Your dad expressing what everyone was thinking certainly helped."

"Yeah…my dad is not one for pretending like things don't matter. I guess after dealing with my mom's parents, he knows what it feels like."

"Well, we've one family down. One to go."

Arriving at Toni's, Gabe parked the truck and walked around to help her down.

"Coming in?" Toni asked.

"No, it's late. I have a lot to do tomorrow in the office since we will be gone next week."

"Okay."

"Toni, thank you for joining me for dinner. It means everything to me."

"You're welcome, babe. They seem like a good crew."

Gabe gently pushed Toni against the front door. Wrapping his arms around her waist, he leaned his head down to kiss her. As usual, this was no quick kiss. Their passion was pure combustion. The kiss left them both wanting more, but knowing that it was too soon for them, they were able to ease back from the fire.

"Good night, Gabe," she whispered.

"Good night, sweetheart."

He waited until she was inside. Walking back to his truck, he had a very satisfied smile on his face. *She's for me. She's for me.*

Saturday morning, while getting ready for Sunday's trip to Chicago, Toni received a three-way call from her sister and brother.

"Hey, Toni," said Alex.

"Hey, Little Brother! What's going on?" Toni asked.

"I'm fine. One second, though. Reecie is on the other line; I'm going to merge the calls," he responded. "Okay, we're all here."

"Hey, Hot Mama! Burning yet?" Reecie teased Toni.

"Girl, you always starting mess!", she exclaimed while she and Alex rolled with laughter. Their sister Reecie was the jokester among them, so they were always going to end up laughing about something.

"What's she talking about?" Alex asked.

"Toni, your sister, is dating a white man. According to her, he is hot, hot, hot!"

"A white dude, Sis?" inquired Alex.

"Yes, he's white, Alex," Toni responded.

"No black guys in San Diego?"

"Trust me; I was not feeling the "white man" thing either. He moves me, though, Alex. Totally and completely unexpected."

"What did your mother say?"

"Oh, Mama doesn't know about him," chimed in Reecie.

"Sherise. Don't make me come to DC," Toni joked. "No, Alex, our mother and father do not know. Frankly, I'm waiting to see how this goes."

"Well, where did you meet him?"

"In a coffee shop."

"Technically, she did not meet him in a coffee shop. She got caught checking him out in a coffee shop, but she met him at his company."

"His company?"

"Yes. His company is a client."

"You dating clients now?" Alex probed.

"No! Yes! Well, I didn't know he was a client when I first saw him, Alex."

"Hmm."

"She went to dinner with him the other night. Been on a few dates, actually," Reecie chimed in, once again.

"Hold on! I am the oldest. I can go where I want and date whom I want. Last I checked, I didn't need anyone's permission."

Reecie and Alex burst into loud laughter. Toni suddenly realized that something was up between the two of them.

"Sis," said Alex, catching his breath. "I already knew about Gabe. You know Reecie can't keep a secret. How she manages to be an attorney with all that client confidentiality stuff is beyond me. Anyway, we decided to call you and give you the business."

"What?!" Toni exclaimed.

"Toni, we had to bother you. You always have a plan. It's nice to see you a bit rattled by this Gabe guy. We had to yank your chain a bit," said Reecie.

"Okay," Toni laughed. "Rest assured, you little bugs, I will get you back. You will not know when it is going to happen, but I will get you back!"

Reecie and Alex laughed, but they knew that Toni would plan her attack. She never let them get away with much when it came to pranks, so they would be on the lookout. They continued catching up with one another, ending the call with their customary "love you" signoffs.

Chapter 11

Toni waited at the airport for Gabe to come around with the rental car. They had left earlier in the afternoon for their week-long trip in Chicago. Both anticipated a very busy week, so they planned to get to their hotel in Northwest Chicago, get something to eat, and go to bed. The office was not far away, but they wanted to be rested.

Gabe pulled up to the curb in the rental SUV, a chocolate-colored Lincoln MKT. He opened the door for Toni and put the bags in the rear cargo space. Having been to the Chicago office many times, he pulled out into the busy airport traffic and made his way to their hotel.

Once there, they checked in at the front desk. Their suites were across the hallway from each other. Gabe tipped the bellman and stood at the door while the bellman placed Toni's bags in the room.

"Dinner in an hour?" he asked her.

"An hour's good. It was a long flight, so I'm going to take a short nap."

"I think I'll do the same," as he leaned over and kissed her softly.

"Hmmm," Toni moaned.

"You are a moaner, woman," he teased.

"Well, when you do what you do so well," she teased him back.

"All right. Let's stop before things get out of hand. See you in a bit," he told her kissing her again.

Both of them enjoyed dinner—amazed at how easy it was to be with each other. They laughed, teased, covered business, and simply appreciated the awe of having met someone that each unreservedly liked.

Walking to the elevator, Gabe kept his hand on Toni's back. Once in the elevator, he leaned down and kissed her, sweeping his tongue into her mouth, showing her just how much he enjoyed their evening. Landing on their floor, he walked her to her door, waved her key over the magnetic panel, opened it, and told her good night. They both needed to be ready for the week, and playing with fire would burn them both.

They met downstairs for breakfast before driving to the office. While traffic was busy, they made it with enough time for Toni to understand the layout of the IT floor. A meeting was scheduled with the IT staff around mid-morning. Because of traffic and other things, APEX offered alternative scheduling. The executives found that allowing employees to come to work at different hours (with some core hours in place) and telecommute assisted them in retention. Turnover could be high in IT. Employees moved for different things. Thankfully, APEX had a stable IT team. The staff stability was good, but they were having problems with quality.

Gabe opened the staff meeting with a few words and an introduction of Toni.

"Team, I would like to introduce Toni Quinn. As you know from my previously communicated email, APEX has hired Ms. Quinn's firm to help us determine what we need to modify in order to get our software releases to a better level of quality. We have had some mishaps, and the upcoming release with Valley Medical has to go smoothly. Toni will be meeting with you at various times. Please make sure your calendars are up-to-date so that she can get some time with you, as needed. Toni, would you like to say something?"

"Thank you, Gabe. First, I would like to tell you that I am impressed by the work you're doing. APEX is really meeting a marketplace need with its software applications, and that is due in part to a good IT organization. Next, as Gabe indicated, I will be scheduling time to meet with some of you. We are here for this week, and our goal is to find out where we can tighten up across the development life cycle in order to get improved results. And last, please call me Toni. For this week, I am located in Conference Room C. You are welcome to drop by, if you like."

"Thanks, Toni. Any questions?"

Gabe and Toni both answered the questions put before them, taking care to let the team know that the goal was improved quality. After the meeting was done, Gabe and Toni walked back to their respective offices to continue the day's work.

The day went quickly. Before either of them knew it, it was well after six o'clock. Considering that they were at the office by seven-thirty that morning and neither had taken a break all day, both Toni and Gabe were tired and hungry, albeit pleased with the results of the day.

Toni had met with a variety of personnel and reviewed any number of documents. She noted that the requirements did not always reference supporting documentation, and in her experience, this helped to clarify the reasons for some of the issues that the team was experiencing with their requirements. Additionally, she saw that the design documentation did not always reference specific require-ments, if there was good design documentation to be found. As a result, everything downstream, including testing could be faulty. While she was not surprised by the findings, she was surprised by the severity of the gaps in their develop-ment processes. She and Gabe would need to talk.

"Hey. You ready to leave?" Gabe asked as he tapped on the conference door and walked inside.

"Yes, give me a minute, please."

Gabe sat in one of the chairs around the table.

"So, how did today go?" he asked.

"Gabe, things are in bad shape. Process-wise, in any case, and that's impacting everything. I think that you need to bring in a team of trainers to retrain and refocus your teams. At the same time, I think you need to look at the timelines you're committing to, particularly when there are a lot of customizations to your products. It appears that you're overcommitting to clients and in doing so, you're causing the teams to take shortcuts and not pay attention to the details. You're getting the product out, but as you know, the rework and warranty fulfillment is eating into your profit and future project timelines."

"Well, that's not what I wanted to hear, but it is what I suspected. We have grown so much in a few years, and we have been running just trying to keep up. I will have to talk with Sam and the other execs about this. I'm sure this will be in your final report, but it sounds like we need to address things with them earlier than the final report."

"Yes, I think so."

"Okay. I'll try to set up some time with them this week."

"All right. Let's go. I'm hungry."

Walking in the garage, Gabe once again put his hand on Toni's back. Suddenly, the fatigue both he and Toni felt took a back seat. The charge felt from his touch had Toni subtly twisting her neck from side-to-side to keep the feelings at bay. *This man*, she thought.

Gabe took a breath. *This woman*, he thought. *I am going to marry her.* For him, it was more than the obvious physical attraction. After getting to know more about her and being in her presence, he appreciated who she was. Her focus. Her drive. Her love for her family and friends. Her spiritual stability. She was it for him. No more looking.

Tuesday was rather busy. The business team, along with a few members of IT, had a video conference with a potential client. Toni sat in on the meeting so that she could get a sense of how they conducted the activities that take place during the early phases of the project.

It did not go well, in her opinion. Questions that should have been asked of the client were not asked, and where the team should have had answers for the client, they did not. At a couple of junctures, Toni stepped in on both sides to help the meeting end successfully. She could see the frustration brewing on both sides.

Gabe called mid-way through the day to ask her to dinner. He wanted to take her to a restaurant he had read about in a local magazine. After reading online reviews, he thought it would be worth the trip. One of the things he and

Toni had in common was their love of good food and a willingness to try new and different cuisines.

At the hotel, Gabe knocked on Toni's door.

She opened the door and took his breath away. *Lord, this woman is fine.*

Toni had selected a red silk St. John surplice blouse that hugged her breasts, offering a generous peek of her enticing cleavage. She paired the blouse with a fitted pair of Tracy Reese pants, matched with some black leather sandals. The black pants curved to her firm thighs, coming to a tight fit at the ankles. She turned around after letting Gabe in, and he almost fainted from the way the pants rested on her behind. *I'm so jealous of these pants right now*, he thought.

"One second, Gabe. Let me put my earrings in and grab my handbag."

She's oblivious to her effect on me right now.

Gabe walked through the suite to stand at the window, while Toni was in the sleeping area finishing her preparations. He took deep breaths trying to calm the rush of the blood in his system. Beads of sweat accumulated on his upper lip, which he slowly wiped away, while thinking about the sexy reason for it walking around in the other room. *Calm down. Just settle down.* That thought went straight out the window, when Toni came walking towards him looking good enough to eat.

He turned from the window to look at her sexy walk. *The woman really knows how to walk.*

"Gabe—," Toni started, but froze at the heat she saw as she looked up into Gabe's eyes.

Gabe let her see just how much he desired her. His eyes and his body said everything he could not get his mouth to say at that moment.

"Gabe—," Toni started again.

He grabbed her hand and pulled her the rest of the way towards him. He backed up to the corner wall that bolstered the floor-to-ceiling windows. He leaned back, turning his head to look out the window. Turning back to her, he breathed, "You are absolutely beautiful."

"Thank you," Toni whispered.

He dropped his hands to her butt and pulled her closer until she rested against him, spreading his long legs so that she had to stand between them. His body wanted to rush, but his head told him to take it slow. He kissed her neck, smelling the sexy perfume she wore. She tilted her neck to the side, her breath catching with the tender kiss. He moved up to her ear, while her hands rested on his shoulders.

"Darling—," Toni sighed.

He skimmed across her face, trying not to mess up her careful application of makeup. He reached her lips.

"You are so sexy," he breathed against them.

Licking her bottom lip, he silently begged for entry. She eased open her lips, swiping the tip of her tongue across his. He took that for the invitation it was.

Gabe brought his hands up across Toni's bottom, over her back, and held his hands at the base of her neck. He swept his tongue inside, telling her with his body how she moved him. Her sexiness was definitely intriguing, but her personality coupled with it made her irresistible.

Toni rested her pelvis against Gabe's while she allowed herself to enjoy the fiery kiss. She moved her hands up his shoulders to put her hands in his hair, massaging his scalp and keeping a grip, lest she slid straight to the floor. His breath caught at the movement and caused him to deepen the kiss, dropping his hands back to her butt, pulling her in tight against his aroused body.

Oh, my, she thought.

Gabe, somehow remembering their dinner appointment—his head swimming and body crying out for release—slowly brought them down from the ride they were on.

Resting his head against hers, he whispered, "I'm sorry for messing up your hair and lipstick. Go ahead and repair it. Okay? We'll go to dinner."

Dazed from the intense encounter, it took Toni a moment to realize what he was saying.

"Ohhhh…"

Gabe turned her around, pointing her in the direction of her bedroom. He couldn't resist running his hand across her bottom again. He felt the shiver that ran through her body and saw her legs shake as she made her way to get ready again.

"Me, too, baby. Me, too," he said as his own legs shook.

Dinner at the new and pricey haute cuisine restaurant was an adventure. The chef experimented with lots of different textures, presentation styles, and flavors. From fancy gelatins to weird meat mixtures, they enjoyed trying the foods, moaning at the delicious ones that set their palates to dancing, and scrunching their noses and shaking their heads at the stuff that had them wondering what the chef could have been thinking.

The meal was perfect for shifting them from the heat-producing scene in Toni's suite and the tension-filled ride downtown.

A much more relaxed ride was had on the way back to their hotel. Walking Toni to her room, Gabe swiped her card, poked his head through the doorway to give her room a scan, and once again left her at the door, thinking of Sam's advice to take it slow.

"Thank you for a lovely evening, Gabe," Toni said.

"You're welcome, love. Have a good night."

He kissed her cheek and walked across the hall to his suite. Closing the door, he leaned against it with one thought. *You got it bad, Man. You really got it bad.*

Wednesday morning dawned with a bit of rain. As Toni prepared for the day, she pondered all that had been happening with her and Gabe. *I am really feeling this man,* she thought once again. It was more than she had expected, and while it seemed as if they had reached a place of contentment with each other rather quickly, it also felt very, very right.

She rolled her computer bag through the doorway of her suite, intending to wait for Gabe in the hall while she checked email on her telephone. After several minutes beyond the time they had agreed to meet, Toni took the few steps to knock on Gabe's door.

Opening the door, Gabe looked like a model out of men's underwear ad, nearly causing Toni to faint right as his feet from his sheer sexiness. Wearing a towel wrapped around his waist, his chest was exposed, showing Toni all that was underneath those well-tailored shirts he had been wearing. *Have mercy! The man is fine!* Gabe rocked a set of abs so keenly defined that all Toni could do was stare at them and the chest that was sprinkled with dark hair that matched that on his head.

With his phone to his hear, he put his hand over the bottom. "I'm sorry," he said softly. "We had an issue this morning with some servers, and I have been on the phone for a bit. Give me a few more minutes. Come in and sit down, please. Help yourself to some tea."

Dazed by the walking Adonis before her, she gestured that he should hold the door open so that she could pull her bag inside. He was already back to the conversation.

Once she was inside, Gabe focused his attention completely on his conference call. She fixed a cup of tea, while watching him pace back and forth between the living and sleeping areas of the suite. He was so consumed with the call that she was sure he was not aware that he was walking around in a towel. *Breathe, Toni, just breathe,* she told herself. *I want him. Yes, I most certainly do.* She took a deep breath and turned her attention to the rain outside and her email account.

Finally, after about another twenty minutes or so, Gabe ended the call. Walking over to Toni, Gabe spoke to her in a tired voice.

"Toni?"

"Yes?"

"My apologies about the delay. Give me a few minutes, and we'll be ready to go."

Setting down her tea, Toni stood up and met Gabe on his way to her. Without saying a word, she ran her hands across the chest that had her thinking all sorts of thoughts for the past half hour. Gabe's breath caught at the contact, at which point he realized that he was still in his towel.

"Oh, babe. I'm sorry. I didn't realize—," he started.

"Hush," Toni whispered. She continued to run her soft hands across his chest and abs, feeling his abs twitch with the contact. She ran her hands up his arms, over his shoulders, and landed with them at the back of his neck. The contrast between his pale skin and her melanin-blessed skin was not lost on her during her exploration. Pulling his head down, she licked his lips and proceeded to kiss him with all the fire that had been burning inside while he had been pacing back and forth in that towel.

"Toni—," Gabe began.

Toni cancelled that sentence by inserting her tongue in his mouth, telling him silently and without shame how much he excited her. She took her time exploring his mouth, moving her hands through his hair and bringing them back down to his well-defined chest. Her body responded in kind—nipples hardening and her sweet place started that humming again.

Gabe had his hands settled on her waist, kissing her back with the passion that had risen like a flame in him upon her touch. *This woman.*

Her hands travelled to the knot in the towel, feeling the developed lower abs he rocked. Her chocolate was melting. Quickly. *This man.*

Gabe stayed her hands, while taking in a deep breath.

"If you go there, we will *not* be going to the office today, sweetheart," he softly told her. "And, as much as I can tell you want me and you can tell that I want you, I think you and I both know that things would change. Besides, I thought you wanted to move slowly."

"Well, I did," she responded in low tones. "You walking around in that towel has me rethinking things."

"I really am sorry about that. I was not thinking about how I was dressed—or, not dressed—just about getting the servers back up."

"Hmm," she said.

""Hmm" what?" he asked.

"Hmm…if you plan to go to work today, you better go get dressed. Otherwise, you will be calling in. For. The. Entire. Day."

His eyes darkened even more at that. He kissed her again, and very wisely turned her around towards her chair.

"I'll be back in few minutes."

Toni cleared her throat.

"Toni?" Gabe called.

"Yeah?" she said.

"We will get to this. I promise you. And, you will be able to do whatever you want."

Toni's temperature spiked again. *Fiddlesticks! I need to change my panties!*

"Hmm. Gabe, I need to go to my room for something. I'll be right back," she said as she quickly made her way out of his suite to her own in order to changed her soaked lingerie.

The day went by rather quickly. The meeting with executives resulted in some strategy changes to help improve quality. Toni was asked to locate some consultants through her firm. They were going to work with the business and IT personnel to start implementing some of Toni's recommendations, mainly those that would have an immediate impact on the quality of the documentation produced.

Some tough conversations and a few arguments were had; after all, IT was Gabe's area, and that is where they were experiencing problems. At some point in the day, behind closed doors and with no one around, he and Toni addressed one of the more pressing issues. They were not on the same page, and the conversation became rather heated.

"Do what you want to do, Gabe," snapped Toni.

"Hold it. It's not about me doing what I want to do. I am the VP of IT, so I know what I can do. After all, I am also a partner in this firm. I am asking you what you think and looking at that in various ways because the changes you are recommending will have an impact. I have an obligation to do so, Toni."

Toni took a calming breath and said, "You're right. I apologize for getting testy."

"Forgiven. Just continue to work with me, please. You have more experience doing this type of initiative than I do, and I respect that, but I still have to ask the questions."

"Okay."

They continued the discussion, ending on a better note.

They had dinner together that evening, careful not to overindulge the wild passion brewing between them—especially, from that morning, which probably accounted for Toni's testiness—and allowing each other to fully process the activities and words spoken that day.

Toni and Gabe were both more convinced about this newfound love. With an opportunity to learn more about each other, they knew that this was it. This was *that love*. Lifetime love.

Chapter 12

"We're coming to visit you," said Regina on the phone the Saturday after Toni's return to San Diego.

"You are? When are you planning to come?" asked Toni.

"Next weekend. Your daddy forgot that he had a couple of airline vouchers expiring. We figured that we would come see you. We saw Reecie the other month when she snuck into town—don't think I don't realize y'all keeping secrets from me, either. We saw Alex the other night when his team was here playing the Orlando Crushers. So, it's your turn."

"Well, a good thing I didn't have anything planned. How long will you be staying?"

"Four days. We get in Thursday night and will fly out Monday night."

"Okay. I will be working Thursday, so you will need to let yourselves in. I'll work a half-day Friday. Maybe, Saturday we can have dinner with someone I would like you to meet."

"Oh, someone like whom?" Regina queried.

"A guy I have been seeing."

"Hmm. I'll let Darryl know so he'll be ready."

"Ready for what, Mama? He's just meeting him."

"Your daddy will have his questions ready. He needs to be prepared."

"Oh, you mean that you will have your questions ready for Daddy to ask, don't you? Tell the truth," she joked with her mother.

"Well, this is the first man in a long time that you have wanted to introduce to us."

"Mama, he's a good man. I think you will like him."

"We'll see. Love you much. Bye, sweetheart."

"Bye, Ma."

Toni tapped the off button on her cellphone and continued dusting in the house. She was going out to dinner later that evening with Gabe, Sam, and his wife Denni, who she'd yet to meet.

Later, while picking out her clothes for her date, she realized that she did not have much time as Gabe would be at her house in about forty-five minutes. *I really should have stopped reading that novel,* she thought.

She quickly picked out a pair of jeans and a loose, sheer silk blouse. She looked sexy and casual. They were going to the harbor to have dinner at a low-key seafood restaurant.

The doorbell rang. *He's here.* She opened the door while putting in her earring.

"Hi, babe. Give me one minute," she said as she reached up to give him a quick kiss and started to turn away.

"Hi. You know better than that. You're going to have to put on some more lipstick."

Gabe kissed Toni as if it had not been less than twenty-four hours since he had last seen her. Toni gladly leaned into the kiss. Finally, Gabe released her.

"Now, go repair your lipstick, so we can go."

"Hmm," as she walked away to the bathroom to repair her lipstick and grab her handbag.

In Gabe's Mercedes coupe, they flew down the highway on the way to the San Diego harbor. He drove fast, but it did not bother her since she drove fast, as well. She was with her man, and that was all that mattered.

Sam and Denni were waiting at the restaurant in the downstairs waiting area looking at the new selection of photos that the restaurant showcased each month. To promote local artists, the restaurant rotated paintings and photographs with prices to encourage purchase. It was a great way to introduce both new and established artists to restaurant patrons.

"Hey, Sam. Hey, Denni," Gabe greeted them, as he walked in holding Toni's hand.

"Hey, Man," said Sam while giving Gabe their usual bro-hug.

"Hi, Gabe," Denni said as she gave him a hug.

"Hi, Denni. May I introduce Toni Quinn? Toni, this is Denni Lawson, Sam's wife and my good friend."

Shaking Toni's hand, Denni told her, "I have heard a lot about you. It is a pleasure to finally meet you."

"Thank you, and it is a pleasure to meet you, as well."

"Well, I'm hungry," announced Sam.

"Man, you're always hungry," said Gabe.

"Look who's talking. The only reason we haven't seen your feet under our table lately is because of Toni."

Toni blushed and laughed along with the rest of them. It was good to know that Gabe had good friends.

They walked upstairs and were immediately seated. While the restaurant was low-key, reservations were recommended since diners tended to linger in the easy atmosphere.

They all enjoyed a relaxed and delicious dinner. They all clicked—cracking jokes, telling funny stories, and getting to know each other. With Sam and Gabe being friends for so long, they had plenty of stories. Some of the things they had gotten up to over the years were quite funny and interesting—making for good tales.

As they all walked outside, Sam and Gabe each holding their ladies' hands, they decided to take a walk along the harbor wall.

Releasing their partners' hands, the men decided to walk together, and the ladies walked together a bit ahead of them.

"He really likes you," Denni told Toni.

"I really like him, Denni. I never thought our chance encounter in the coffee shop would lead us here months later."

"Well, strange things happen. Sam and I actually met in the airport. I bumped into him, spilling my hot Starbucks chai tea latte over him—completely ruining his shirt. Thankfully, his shirt took the brunt of it!"

"Oh, my! What happened?"

"I apologized. Profusely. I was so embarrassed! He was cool about it, but I could tell he was annoyed. He told me that he had another shirt, but he would only accept my apology if I accepted a date with him. I didn't know if he lived in the city, so I flippantly told him, "Sure!" Little did I know that he was going to whip out his business card, ask me for my number, and call me the next day to arrange the date."

"That was fast."

"Yes, it was. We almost missed the beauty of what we had, but we finally got our minds right, as my grandmother says. Five years ago; we have been married for three years."

"Wow. What a love story!"

"Yes, it is, I must admit."

"My parents are visiting next weekend. Would you and Sam like to join me and Gabe for dinner on Saturday? My friend Karen and her husband, Allan, will be there, as well."

"We don't have anything planned. I'll ask Sam to be sure."

"Okay. I'll be cooking at my home."

Turning around, Denni asked Sam, "Honey, do we have anything planned for next Saturday evening? Toni's parents are going to be in town, and she's invited us to dinner."

"Sounds good to me," he responded.

"Saturday, it is," Denni told Toni.

"Great! I look forward to having you."

Gabe smiled at the ease at which his friends and Toni communicated. Sam was a brother to him and Denni a sister, as well, so how they got along was just as important to him as his natural sisters and brothers-in-law.

On the way home, Gabe held Toni's hand over the console.

"What are you doing tomorrow afternoon?" he asked.

"I've got some paperwork to do. I am putting in a proposal for another client. I have done some work with them before, and they're thinking about sourcing another engagement."

"Oh, sounds good. I hope it goes well."

"I do, too. They should be ready to start by the time I'm wrapping up the APEX engagement. So, great timing on my end."

Pulling into Toni's driveway, Gabe turned off the car. Hands on the steering well, he turned towards Toni.

"Toni."

"Yes?"

"I love you."

"Hmm?"

"I love you. It may seem sudden, but I do."

"You really don't do the "great build-ups", do you?"

"What for? We're grown. I know what I think and feel. No need to play around. I don't do games."

"And, I appreciate that."

"I just wanted you to know that I'm thinking long-term."

"Hmm. That's nice to know."

"Good," sighed Gabe.

"Gabe?"

"Yeah, babe?"

"I love you, too."

Gabe raised an eyebrow at Toni's admission. He hadn't told her so that she could tell him the same in return. He simply wanted her to know what he was thinking about her, how he felt. He was humbled by her declaration. *I'm going to marry her*, he thought once again.

He wrapped his hand around her neck and brought her forward to seal their love with a kiss so powerful it made them both catch their breaths.

Gabe ended the kiss and walked Toni to her front door.

"Good night, Toni."

"Coming in for a few?"

"Not tonight, sweetheart," Gabe said regretfully.

"Okay."

"I'll call you when I get home."

Toni kissed him good night. He waited until he heard the lock click.

In his car, he told the voice recognition system to call Sam.

"Hey," Sam answered.

"Sam, I need a ring."

"What? A wedding ring?"

He heard Denni's voice in the background, "Who needs a wedding ring?"

"Woman, this is two grown men talking," Sam teased.

"Gabe?" Denni asked after taking the phone from Sam and putting it on speaker.

"Yeah, Denni?"

"Are you going to propose to Toni?"

"Yes, I am."

"Congratulations!"

"Yeah, congratulations! Now, my grocery bill will go down!" Sam said through the phone while laughing.

"Not quite. We'll both come to dinner!"

"Anytime, my brother. That's a good woman. Not like mine, but still good, though," he continued to tease him.

"You know it," said Denni, kissing Sam while Gabe could hear.

"Okay. Time for me to go. Y'all trying to get nasty again. Love y'all," he said.

"Don't hate. We love you, too," Sam and Denni said together.

"'Night."

"Good night, Gabe. We're happy for you," said Sam.

Chapter 13

Toni rushed around her home trying to make sure everything was ready for the evening's dinner with her parents and friends.

Her parents had gone out earlier in the day to visit with some friends of theirs who lived in Del Mar. They were now back and resting in their room. While Regina had asked if she could help, Toni told her mom that she had things covered.

Karen and Allan were on their way. Allan was bringing a couple of his delicious sweet potato pies, so she did not have to do dessert. She had some homemade vanilla ice cream, and that would do fine.

The doorbell rang.

"Hello, Carina! Hello, Allan!"

"Hey, Love!" Karen said, giving Toni a hug. Allan followed behind with a bag in his hand. He gave Toni a hug with his free hand.

"I'm so glad you're here! I am so nervous!" Toni exclaimed.

"Nothing to be nervous about, Love. It will all go well."

"This is the first time that Gabe is meeting my parents and meeting y'all. I just want everything to go well."

"It will. Come on. Let's put the pie in the kitchen and get you something to drink."

"Yes, I'm thirsty and tired of standing in the doorway," teased Allan.

"Oh, I'm soooo sorry!"

"No problem, Girl. You know I'm just teasing you."

"Allan, leave her alone. Stop playing," said Karen.

"Woman, leave me alone," Allan said patting Karen's butt and kissing her on the nose.

A few minutes later the doorbell rang again. By this time, Toni's parents were downstairs chatting with Karen and Allan who they had met several times before.

Toni went to answer the door.

"Hi, Gabe."

"Hi, Sweetheart." He leaned down to give her a light kiss.

"Hmm. Just what I needed."

"Why? What's wrong?"

"Nothing really. I'm just a little nervous."

"Everything will be fine. Relax."

Toni took a deep sigh. "Okay."

She walked Gabe to the sitting room where everyone was gathered.

"Dad, Mom. I'd like to introduce Gabriel Jackson. Gabe, my parents, Darryl and Regina Quinn."

"Nice to meet you, Sir. Nice to meet you, Ma'am."

"A pleasure to meet you, Gabe," Darryl responded.

"A pleasure and a surprise," said Regina, being her usual candid self.

The doorbell rang again. Toni went to answer it. Sam and Denni were there.

"Hi! Come on in, please. Welcome!"

"Hi, Toni," Denni said.

"Hi, Toni. I feel like I'm seeing you every day," Sam joked.

"I know!" Toni laughingly said. "Follow me."

"Everyone. This is Sam and Denni. They are great friends of Gabe. Sam and Gabe went to college together."

Introductions were made all around. Soon, Toni led them to the dining room which was at the rear of the house overlooking the backyard. It was an addition to the house that the previous homeowners had made in order to modernize and make the home more useful and appealing to buyers. Toni fell in love with the large dining room and renovated kitchen during the home tour. Upon seeing both, it sealed the deal for her.

With the long natural wood table that seated ten people, there was plenty of space for them. They all sat down. As was custom in Toni's family, a short prayer of thanks was given for the meal, and they all started passing around dishes.

"So, Gabe," said Regina.

Toni cleared her throat, but Regina ignored her, cutting her eyes at her just a bit.

Lord, help us, Toni thought.

"Gabe. Toni didn't tell us you were white. Not that it's a problem, but it is a surprise."

"Well, Ma'am, yes, I am. Not much I can do about it," he teased.

"Cheeky, aren't you?" Regina joked.

"Regina, leave the man alone. Toni's grown," chimed Darryl.

"She may be grown, but she's still my baby."

"That is funny, Mrs. Quinn. My mother said the same thing when she met Sam," Denni interrupted.

Sam picked up his wife's lead and said, "She sure did. She told me that Denni was her baby. "My only child" she said and that she was not playing about her. I got her point."

Everyone laughed.

"There is really no need to beat around the bush, in my opinion," continued Regina. "Toni is black, and Gabe is white. That is not exactly a great recipe for relationship success. Folks still think some kind of way about cross-cultural couples."

"Mama, we have considered the obstacles. We decided that we would deal with them as they come."

"Humph."

"Regina, you don't just have to look on the bad side. There are some good relationships like theirs, and you know it," said Darryl.

"Yeah, but those relationships don't involve one of my children."

Darryl grabbed her hand. He realized that she had seen things in her lifetime that the younger people at the table had not seen, and that those things concerned her.

As her husband's touch soothed her, Regina relented by saying, "Gabe, it is a pleasure to meet you, but you will find that I don't mince words. This is my daughter, and since she's introduced you to us, that means something to me."

"I understand, Mrs. Quinn. It means something to me, as well. I would never intentionally harm Toni or put her in harm's way."

Regina was quiet as she contemplated what Gabe had told her.

"Okay, now that we've got that out of the way, let's enjoy the rest of the meal. Allan, Karen told me that you brought some of your sweet potato pie," Darryl said to the group.

"Yes, Sir, I did. I knew you were coming. I also know that you think my pie is the best in the world. I didn't want to disappoint you," he joked.

"Honey, you need to take three seats with that," said Karen joining in the joking.

"Woman, you know I can throw down with some pie."

"Uh huh."

Allan leaned over and whispered in her ear. She blushed.

"Uh huh. I thought so," said Allan.

"Oh, boy. Here we go," said Toni.

"Looks like a bit of these two here," responded Gabe, waving one of his hands in the direction of Sam and Denni.

"Hush," teased Denni.

They all laughed. Each couple had a good, healthy relationship. They didn't get there without some tests and trials, but they were still in love with their mates. They knew that the first blushes of love would be tested, but also that the tests could be passed if the couple were willing to try.

Dinner finished in good spirits. Everyone moved out to the back porch for some pie and drinks. It was a good, clear evening, so they just sat and chatted with one another.

"Gabe, why don't you come in with me to get some more ice," requested Darryl.

"Okay."

"Oh, dear. What is daddy going to say," asked Toni as she saw them walk towards the kitchen.

"You know your daddy was going to say something— no matter what I said. He was going to ask his own questions," said Regina.

They all laughed while wishing they could hear the conversation between the two men.

Darryl had the ice bucket with him, and Gabe stood next to him by the refrigerator.

"Now, Gabe, regardless of how I mess with my wife, Toni is still my daughter."

"Yes, Sir."

"That being said, I simply expect you to treat her well. Whether this goes the distance or not, I still expect you to treat her well. Understand?"

"Yes, I do. We love each other, Sir. In fact, I would like to marry her."

"What?"

"I would like to marry her. I would like to ask your and Mrs. Quinn's permission, if I may."

"Why so soon?"

"Sir, we have known each other for a bit of time. More than that, I don't need to look anymore. I knew shortly after our second meeting that I was going to marry her."

"Well, you got guts, I'll say that. One second," he said. He called to Regina, "Gina, come here for a sec."

Regina came into the kitchen not knowing what to expect. Darryl was easygoing, but he was tough when it came to his children. She wasn't sure what had been said between the two men.

"Regina, Gabe here has something he wants to say."

"Mrs. Quinn. Sir. I love Toni. With your permission, I would like to ask her to marry me."

"How long—," Regina started.

"Honey, it's okay," Darryl said.

"But, you haven't known her very long," Regina insisted.

"He says he knew after their second meeting."

"Well!"

"Gina, you okay with this?"

"I have my reservations, quite honestly, but I can tell that Toni loves you. We have never seen her so affectionate with anyone. You're good for her. Just love my daughter, or you will hear from me," she said firmly.

"Yes, Ma'am. Sir, thank you."

"Son, you're welcome. Treat her right."

"I most certainly will. She's got my heart."

They returned to the porch. The rest of the group looked up to see what the mood was. All three faces were blank, but Sam looked at Gabe. Gabe gave him a slight nod. Sam grabbed Denni's hand and gave it a squeeze after giving Gabe a smile. Only they knew that Gabe was going to ask her parents about marrying Toni.

While a lot of couples made the decision to marry and then told their parents of the decision, Gabe's brothers-in-law had asked his parents about his sisters, and he saw how much it meant to his parents. He wanted Toni's parents to have the same respect, especially since she was the first one of their children to get married.

The dinner wrapped up a bit later. Everyone told Toni that they had enjoyed a great time and that they must do it again. New friendships had begun between Toni's and Gabe's friends, so it was a good thing at the end of the day.

Gabe stayed behind to help Toni clean up. Her parents went upstairs to give them some time alone. Darryl had hugged him and so had Regina. This surprised him, but he was very thankful for their acceptance and demonstrated affection. He realized that they loved their daughter, and like his parents, wanted their child to be treated well.

"So, I think things went well, don't you?" he asked Toni.

"I do. What did my father say?"

"He told me to treat you well."

"That's it?"

"Pretty much. Your mom threatened to break a couple of bones. I don't think she's over the fact that I'm white—not just yet, anyway."

"What?" she exclaimed.

"Just kidding. Well, not on the white thing. She basically told me the same thing—to treat you well."

"Hmm," Toni said with a slight frown on her forehead.

"Come here," Gabe said pulling Toni towards him. "Look. They are your parents and care for you. If they didn't say anything, I would be surprised."

"I know, Gabe. Still."

"Rest assured that my parents did the same thing with my brothers-in-law. And, so did I."

"What!" she exclaimed.

"Marian and Allison are my sisters. I love them, and Brian and Patrick needed to know that I wasn't playing."

"Well, put like that..."

"Exactly. Now, give me a kiss. All these folks here tonight meant that I couldn't kiss you in the way that I wanted to."

"Is that so?"

"You better know it."

Toni tilted her head back. Gabe teased the sensitive skin of her neck, easing up to her hotspot located behind her ear.

"Umm," moaned Toni.

""Umm" is right," whispered Gabe.

He reached her lips and gave her a kiss that showed her how much he wanted her. Toni opened her mouth with the familiarity gained over the past weeks. *This man can really kiss.*

Gabe pulled her in closer, holding onto her face by both hands while he leaned into the kiss. He slid his hands down her body, easing his hands under her top. His fingers flicked the tips of her breasts causing her to shiver with arousal. She felt heat shoot from her nipples to her core—causing it to throb and her juices to start flowing.

"Gabe. Baby. I can't—," Toni cautioned, although her body was saying something else entirely. *This man makes me feel so sexy.*

"You taste so good," he said, increasing the pressure of both the kiss and his hands on her nipples.

"Like Allan's sweet potato pie," she whispered with a smile in her voice.

"You just had to go and ruin the moment," he laughed.

"Well, you were going in, and my parents are upstairs," she laughed.

"You're right," he said, sliding his hands from underneath her blouse. He tapped her on her behind. "This isn't the time. Speaking of time, Allison wanted to me to extend an invitation to her baby shower that is weekend after next. She has already put the invite in the mail, as well. I am almost finished with the crib that you saw earlier this week, and I will deliver it to her at the shower."

"Oh, that's thoughtful of her. I'm free, so I will be more than happy to attend."

"Okay. Let's finish up. I'll let you get some rest. It's been a busy day."

"Yes, but a good one. Gabe, I love you."

"I love you, too, Toni." He kissed her again.

They finished cleaning. Toni walked him to the door.

"You're a good man, you know that?"

"Now that you tell me, I do," he joked.

"Really."

"Well, it means a lot coming from you, Baby."

"Drive safely."

"Will do."

Toni watched him from the doorway. *I'm going to marry that man.*

While Gabe and Toni were downstairs dealing with their own passions, a different kind of conversation was occurring upstairs between her parents.

"Darryl," said Regina.

"Yes, Gina," responded Darryl, walking out of the ensuite bathroom, with a towel draped around his neck and another wrapped around his waist.

"Don't "Yes, Gina" me, Darryl Quinn. You know full well what's up. And, you can cut out the sexy eye look. You need to put on a robe. I'm not falling for it!"

"You know good and well the only reason I packed that robe is because we're here with Toni. You haven't seen a robe since Alex permanently left home and unless we have guests. Now, Gina, what's wrong?" he asked, moving to sit beside her on the window bench. He gently moved her head to rest on his shoulder.

"What's wrong? Really, Darryl? You know exactly what I need to talk about! This is Toni—my baby. My first. And? A white man?"

"Baby, the man loves her. A sightless man could see that. And, a blind woman could sense that Toni thinks the same about him. Am I surprised? Yes, I am. I didn't expect any of my children to marry anyone who isn't black. Frankly, I took for granted that love would look like them; that it would look like me, look like you."

"I wish she would marry someone black. It would be easier."

"How do you know that, Gina? Do you know something about black men that says they'll always do what's right towards our black daughters, making it easier? If you do, then it would be something that I don't know. Don't forget I have a cousin whose husband—whose black husband—wiped out hundreds of thousands of dollars from their business and personal accounts causing her to have to start over again," he asked. "Further, you and I know that no matter how compatible and alike two people are, life will bring something that challenges that love. And, more than once."

"She could wait. For a black man," she whispered.

"How long, Gina?" he softly asked. "She's almost forty years old. How long should she wait to meet a black man who will treat her right?"

"The world is not fair, Darryl," she whispered again.

"No, it's not, Sweetheart. But, you know what's made it worthwhile? Having the love of a good woman with whom I could share the trials. Gabe is a wise man. Our daughter is a good woman. I, for one, couldn't be happier about his selection."

"Am I being selfish?" Gina softly inquired.

"No, baby. You're being a mother. Why don't you talk to her?"

"I probably should."

Tilting her head towards him and kissing her softly, Darryl responded, "And when you come back, I'm gonna be right here minus this towel so you can be as selfish as you want."

"Really, Darryl?"

"Really, Gina. You know I am not playing. I'll always want you. That's the kind of love you and I have. Now, go see her, and hurry back," swatting her on the behind after she stood.

She deep-kissed her husband of more than three decades, boldly placing her hand between the folds of his towel, letting him know that she would always want him, too.

Toni walked up the stairs after securing the house for the night. She smiled in thankfulness for the night having gone well between everyone. Two families down. Upon hearing that Toni's parents were coming into town, Gabe had arranged lunch with his parents for the following day so that both sets of parents could be introduced. *What a weekend*, Toni thought.

"Toni?", her mom called to her from the doorway of the guestroom.

"Yes, Mama?"

"Got a second, baby, for a chat?" asked Regina.

"Certainly. Come on into my bedroom."

Walking down the hall to Toni's room, Gina sat in one of the chairs in the sitting area. Regina turned to Toni, gently taking one of her hands in hers.

"What is it, Mama?" Toni inquired.

"Toni," Regina started. "You are my first baby. When you were born, your daddy and I were so happy, if truthfully scared, about the little person that was our responsibility. It didn't matter that we had nine-plus months—you took your time coming here—to get ready and adjust, we were still in awe of the gift and responsibility before us. So, we were careful with you. Tried to get it right. Although you are a grown woman, a successful adult—we couldn't be prouder of you and your sister and brother—I still have the same care for you—each of you, in fact. Your happiness is important to me. Concerning Gabe, where do you see this going?"

"Ma, I love him. I never would have guessed that I would be dating him. I'm strictly chocolate—well, I was."

"What is "strictly chocolate"? Regina quickly asked.

"You know. Chocolate. Only black men."

"What the—?" Regina asked, bursting into laughter. "Strictly chocolate, huh? Well, Gabe must be white chocolate? Wait until I tell Darryl." She continued to chuckle, shaking her head at her oldest child.

Toni joined in with Regina's laughter.

"Oh, Mama. Believe me, I was arrested by the attraction. I had to stop and think hard about whether love had to come in a certain color. Or, if I was more interested in being able to give and receive love. Gabe gives and receives. I give and receive. We complement each other, strange as it may seem. Very unexpected, Mama, but I am happy."

"The world can be cruel, Toni. Be very certain about this. Things can be difficult enough with people who are of the same culture. Love ain't about feelings. Feelings change. Some days, I *feel* like I love your daddy so much, I could just eat him up. Other days, he makes me wonder what I was thinking so many years ago. Yet, Toni, each day, he and I make a *decision* to love one another. It is why, all these years later, we are still together. Loving Gabe will have to be a daily decision. Even on those days when you don't feel like being in the same house, on the same darn street, in the same—."

"I get it, Mama," Toni laughed.

Grinning from ear-to-ear, Regina pulled her oldest daughter to her, putting her head on her shoulder. She missed holding her children, especially with them living away from home, so if she got a chance, she gave them one of her serious mother hugs.

Patting Toni's head, she told her, "It is clear to me that you love Gabe. I hope things go well for you, sweetheart."

"Thanks, Mama, I do, too. I love you."

"Love you, too, baby."

Chapter 14

The baby shower took place a couple of weekends after the dinner party. Toni selected a gift from the registry, balancing the new relationship between her and Allison as she saw fit, considering she was the mother-to-be's brother's girlfriend.

Dressed in a gauzy, yellow sundress that looked fabulous against her chocolate-toned skin paired with strappy sandals of the same color and her hair in an Afro puff, Toni looked fresh and like a woman in love. She arrived at the restaurant in which the hostesses, Marian and one of Allison's close friends, had reserved a private room for the celebration. Walking into the large room, she saw a lot of faces that she did not know; however, she did see Ellen, Gabe's mother, and Denni, Sam's wife.

"I'm so glad you could come, Toni," greeted Ellen, being gracious as always. She hugged Toni in genuine affection. Toni and Gabe had shared dinner again with his parents and siblings, helping the relationship to blossom. Although Toni did not know, Gabe had told his parents that he planned to ask Toni to marry him, and they could not be happier about his choice in a life partner.

"Glad I could make it," answered Toni.

"I'm going to greet some of the others," Ellen said. "Looks like Denni is on her way over." She hugged her before departing.

"Hey, Denni," Toni cheerfully said with a hug.

"Hey, Girl," said Denni. "Trust Marian to do a baby shower like a wedding reception. I have to admit, though, that it is gorgeous."

"Yes, it is. It really is. Excuse me for a minute. All that water I had this morning is catching up with me."

"Go ahead. I'll be here somewhere in the throng."

While in the restroom stall, Toni heard two chatting women enter the restroom.

"Did you see her?" asked one of the women with a high-pitched voice.

"Yes. Can you believe he's dating her?" asked the other woman.

"No, I can't. Seriously. What is he thinking? A man in his position? Gabe has a social image to keep up."

"I hear that she has her own consulting firm."

"Yes, but still..." responded the woman.

"You know Gabe has never been concerned about social stuff. You probably scared him off talking about marriage all the time."

"Well, I still think we would make a great couple."

Coming out of the stall, Toni went to the sink to wash her hands.

"Ladies, good afternoon."

"Oh, hi," they responded rather insincerely, clearly surprised by her presence.

Unknown to either of them, Marian came out of another stall.

"Kimberly. Charlotte," she said while washing her hands. "I see some things haven't changed. Cattiness still seems to be your agenda of the day. By the way, have you met Toni? She's Gabe's girlfriend."

"Ladies," Toni repeated in a very disinterested tone.

"For the record, we, Gabe's family, happen to think that Gabe has made an *excellent* choice in Toni. We all hope he's wise enough to marry her. He couldn't do better, in our opinion. Have a good afternoon. Enjoy the shower."

Marian lightly put her hand on Toni's arm leading her out of the restroom.

"Toni, I'm so glad Gabe got rid of that gold-digger Kimberly! Her family did business with dad for a number of years. That is why she's here."

"Well, I'm sure he had his reasons."

"He did. I, for one, am glad he saw through her schemes."

"You didn't have to say anything, you know. They weren't of concern to me. I know where Gabe's interests lie," Toni said with a wink.

"I knew my brother was smarter than he looks," Marian laughed. "It's been a pleasure getting to know you. Let's enjoy this shower. I can't imagine what I was thinking with all this stuff!"

Chapter 15

Time passed with work being very busy for the couple. They were in the height of a SoCal summer—nice temps and sunshine. Toni was coming towards the end of her engagement with APEX. Thankfully, the changes she recommended were implemented, and they saw noticeable change in the decrease of document defects and software defects. The Valley Medical work went out, and although, some rework was needed, it was in much better shape than what was expected upon Toni's initial inspection.

With the moderate slow-down in work—at least from the perspective of the work being done by Toni's firm— Gabe decided that it was ideal timing to ask Toni to marry him. She had been awarded the engagement with her other client, so she had no time for a break.

Gabe asked her to dinner via text while they were both at work.

Hey, Babe. Dinner tonight? - **Gabe**

Hey. Sure. What time? - **Toni**

How's seven-thirty? - **Gabe**

That'll work. Where? - **Toni**

There's a great place in La Jolla that I want to go to tonight. I'll pick you up. - **Gabe**

Dress code? - **Toni**

Semi-dressy - **Gabe**

Sure thing. Love you. - **Toni**

Love you, too. - Gabe

Gabe took the stairs down to Sam's office. Sam was leaving early; Denni was going to a cousin's baby shower in DC for the weekend.

"Hey, Sam."

"Hey, Gabe. Tonight's the night, huh?"

"Yes. I can't believe it, but I'm actually nervous. What if she says no?"

"Man, that woman is not going to say no. Y'all have had arguments—big ones—and she's still around. She *ain't* going to say no. Denni says she ain't saying no, and you know my baby is almost always right. Don't tell her I said that last part," he laughed.

"You better hope I don't," Gabe teased. "I want this to go well, you know?"

Sam came around his desk, grabbing his briefcase at the same time. He slapped Gabe on the shoulder.

"It will, my friend. Relax." He walked with Gabe towards the door.

"Shawna, I'm gone for the weekend. Have a good one."

"You, too, Sam. Tell Denni hi."

"Will do."

"Bye, Shawna," said Gabe.

"Bye, Gabe. Have a good weekend."

At the elevator, Sam turned to Gabe.

"Relax. Call me tonight."

"Okay."

Gabe was at Toni's shortly before seven-thirty. He took a couple of minutes to calm down. Toni was usually ready. She told him that she was running a few minutes behind due to some problems at the dry cleaners earlier.

Calm down, he told himself. *She's going to say, "Yes".*

He walked to the door and rang the doorbell. While he had a key to Toni's home, he still rang the doorbell.

"Hey, Babe," Toni said when she opened the door. She was wearing a knee-length royal blue dress that hugged her in all the right places.

"Hey," Gabe said giving her a light kiss, trying to keep his mind on one thing at a time, while the dress was talking to him. *I've got to make her my wife. Soon.*

"Something to drink?"

"No, I'm okay."

"Well, I'm ready. I got back sooner than I thought. I can't believe they ruined my blouse," as she locked up the house.

"What did they say?" as he opened the SUV door for her.

"They are going to have the manager call me. Call me? Clearly, the blouse is ruined. I told them okay."

"They'll make it right, I'm sure."

"I hope so."

They rode in silence with a good romantic mix of music on the stereo. Kem's soulful love ballad "I Can't Stop Loving You" played softly. As normal, Gabe had Toni's had across the console. He gave it a squeeze. She turned her head and smiled at him.

Gabe weaved the vehicle through the seaside town of La Jolla. He pulled up to the valet stand and walked around to Toni's side. He walked her into the Italian restaurant.

"Reservation for Gabe Jackson, please."

"Yes, Sir. We have your table ready."

The hostess sat them at a secluded table per his request. They had a view outside with the setting sun.

"Your server will be right over."

"Thank you."

Gabe pulled out Toni's chair and then sat in his.

The server came and took their drinks order. He returned and received their dinner selections. During this time, they chatted with ease as was normal. A bit of work and a bit of personal were covered. Allison had given birth to a healthy baby girl, which she and Patrick had named Liza Gail Ward. The cradle presented by Gabe at the baby shower made all the women cry—they could see the love that went into its creation. Toni discussed what a delightful and happy baby little Liza was.

They received their meal and proceeded to eat. Their server came to collect their empty plates and asked if they wanted dessert. They both made a selection from the delicious-sounding options.

With desserts on the table, Gabe decided that he should pose his question.

"Toni, before we eat dessert…"

"What's up, Gabe? Something wrong?"

"No," he said, taking a deep breath.

"Okay…"

He rose from his chair and kneeled beside hers.

"Gabe?" Toni whispered.

"Toni, I love you. You are everything that I want and some of what I didn't know I needed. I want to spend my life with you making memories, making love, and making babies. Will you marry me?"

"Oh, Gabe. It would be an honor to be your wife," Toni answered with tears in her eyes. "I love you. I really do."

"Then, that's all I ask."

They kissed with all the passion of a newly engaged couple, completely ignoring the discrete claps of the surrounding diners.

Chapter 16

The reality of Toni and Gabe's cross-cultural relationship hit home during an early fall trip to Napa Valley. Their busy work and social schedules had them going at a pace that was not conducive to a successful relationship, so Gabe proposed a weekend getaway to Napa. They opted for early November to avoid the bulk of the harvest season tourists.

Their multi-room suite at a local bed-and-breakfast afforded them both the space and closeness they needed in their blossoming relationship. The decision to wait on sex was not an easy one for them to make—simply being next to other got their blood to pumping—but it helped them to think clearer in the many discussions they had about joining their lives. They were not young people who were willing to just abandon it all for the sake of love or rather, lust. They had full lives prior to meeting each other—and those lives included assets, patterns of behavior, and all the other things that, if left undiscussed, could mean unnecessary trouble later in their marriage.

Gabe and Toni left their B&B mid-morning on the Saturday of their four-day trip and drove into the center of town to do some browsing and shopping. Relaxed from a delicious breakfast, they strolled while holding hands and making the odd comment about the various wares for sale in the shops. One shop's products caught their attention; they decided to take a closer look by going inside.

The shop was a bit busy. They parted ways to do a bit of separate looking at the unique items. Toni made a selection and went to stand in line. One couple was in line before her at one register and a lone lady was purchasing her items at the other register.

The clerk at the first register was in the middle of finishing the transaction. Gabe had made his way towards Toni with a couple of items in hand for purchase, as he was going to purchase all of their selections. He stopped to browse at one of the nearby impulse purchase displays.

"Sir, may I help you?" the twenty-something white clerk asked him, completely ignoring Toni.

"Excuse me?" he asked.

"May I help you?" she repeated.

Toni turned her head towards Gabe with a look in her eye that he knew quite well. The clerk was about to get a lesson in customer service.

"Well, actually, you can help my fiancée first since she was here before me. Surely, you saw her before I walked up?" he replied very firmly, his green eyes darkening to almost black due to the budding anger.

The clerk swung her head from side-to-side. Since another couple had joined the other line behind the lone lady, they knew that Toni was next in line, as well.

The clerk responded with an eye-roll that was such bad business that it had Gabe softly setting his items on the counter. He removed Toni's items from her hands and set them on the counter, too. He reached for the hand nearest him, intertwining their fingers.

"I do business with establishments that understand that *all* customers deserve excellent service. You can sell these items to someone else," he said with such steeliness that Toni squeezed his hand to calm him.

He turned to lead Toni out of the shop. Toni knew that Gabe was very upset. While they generally had no issues with people, every now and then—perhaps more often than they should in the twenty-first century—they encountered someone with a crappy attitude.

"Babe?" Toni said to him while she led him to a bench to sit down for a moment.

He said nothing, but turned to look at her with the look of a man who would protect his woman from any level of disrespect. He didn't play about Toni. With anyone.

"Babe," she repeated, unlinking their hands and rubbing his back, moving her hands to the nape of his neck to massage it. "It sucks. Believe me, I know. It's not worth being upset. It's an attempt to ruin our day, and I refuse to allow that to happen. I am here with you, and it's okay. We move on, all right?"

"Toni, I am friends with Sam and have been for many years, as you know. We have had some awful encounters during our time, but there is something different about how people view us as a couple. You are going to be my wife, and under no circumstances will I allow you to be mistreated. I am always willing to move on, but I will always address any disrespect towards you that occurs in my presence. Okay?"

"Okay," she whispered. "I love you, Gabe."

"I love *you*, Toni. I don't mind telling the world that I do and that you're mine, either."

She turned his face towards her so that she could kiss her agreement. She *was* his. He was *hers*, as well. *#TeamJackson, I need to get shirts made with that on the front*, she jokingly thought.

Chapter 17

December - Later That Year

Regina bustled around the church's bridal chamber helping Toni get ready for the wedding. After a few quick months of planning—neither Gabe nor Toni were willing to wait any longer than that—they were about to join lives in one of most time-honored (and legal) ways to do so.

"Baby, you look beautiful," she said to Toni.

Toni had designed a champagne-colored wedding gown made of silk with tasteful lace inserts. One of Karen's cousins provided custom-made clothes, and she was able to meet Toni's tight timeline. The gown fit her tall body. The shoulders were a series of spaghetti straps clasped together with a matching set of vintage pins that Regina had found. The back of the gown came halfway up her back, while strands of rhinestones draped from the shoulder straps to cover the top of her back. With her matching veil of silk and lace, she was absolutely one beautiful bride. The joy of being a woman loved by her man was written all over her face. She practically glowed. There was no doubt about her decision to marry Gabe.

"You really do, Sis. Gabe's jaw is going to drop," said Reecie, looking good in her navy maid-of-honor gown. "That gown says, "Strip me" - in a not-so-sleazy way. It's gonna be on like popcorn to-night!" she further exclaimed, snapping her fingers in the air. The other women burst into laughter at Reecie's antics.

"Hush, with your fast self," said Regina, with a smile in her voice. "Toni does not need you talking smack right now. In any case, she's her mama's child. She knows what to do. Why you think your daddy is always smiling?"

"Mama, that is TMI," said Reecie.

"It sure is, Mama," agreed Toni.

"Y'all need to quit. Y'all know you didn't come from underneath a rock," Denni laughingly said. She was one of the matrons of honor. Denni and Toni had become very good friends, making the men in their lives quite pleased. Consequently, Denni had spent plenty of time with Toni and her sister, who she also considered to be a good friend.

"Ain't that right," said Marian. She wasn't in the wedding, but was sitting in on the bridal party preparations. She and Brian were going to have a baby. A big surprise to them after years of deciding that they were not going to have children and too busy to do anything else about it. Well, apparently, not that busy, since she was two months pregnant. At forty-two years of age, she was being rather careful to help ensure a good pregnancy and delivery.

Allison was still breast-feeding, but she was a matron of honor, as well. Along with her, Patrick was participating in the wedding; he, as a groomsman.

"It makes the world go 'round, right?" Allison queried, smiling like a woman who knew what she was talking about.

"Yes, sweetheart, it sure does," said Regina.

The wedding consultant came in. "Okay, we're ready. Let's do this." Marian scooted out to take her place next to her husband Brian who was already seated on the groom's side.

The music started, and the party made its way down the aisle. At the front of the sanctuary, Gabe stood with Sam, as his best man. Toni's brother Alexander joined as an additional groomsman.

Toni and Gabe had chosen another song in lieu of the traditional wedding march. She walked to Raheem DeVaughn's "Infiniti". Visions407, the live band that they had hired for the reception, was also performing the ceremony music, and they did a wonderful job of covering the intimate song about a couple's enduring love.

Gabe looked at Toni as if all he needed was coming towards him. Indeed, it was. Their love was sweet, yet strong. It was passionate, yet pure in its authenticity. It was clear to their families and friends. They knew that no matter what, they saw before them two people who would fight for their love.

Their vows were stated with all the passion and sincerity of two people who understood the magnitude and significance of the life exchange they were making. The kiss that sealed the exchange was as hot as expected, even raising a few brows from the attendees!

The reception was held at a swanky event center in a nearby town. Everyone had a great time — toasts to the new couple, dancing, great music, and excellent food. Soon, though, it was time for the newly married couple to depart.

Gabe stood up, reaching for the hand of his new bride so that she could rise, too. He leaned down to tell Sam that they were going to leave. He then signaled to the Master of Ceremonies, who made the announcement. The guests lined up near the entrance with their bubbles while Gabe and Toni hugged their family and friends.

The guests blew bubbles as the couple walked by. Gabe seated Toni in his coupe. They stopped at Gabe's home—now Toni's home—to change clothes.

He carried her across the threshold, kissing her passionately as he let her down to walk on her own. They walked through the spacious mid-century-like home—for it was a modern home in mid-century style—to get to the bedroom. Toni had moved her items into the house over the past month, opting to keep her property for rental purposes.

Reaching the bedroom, Gabe helped Toni remove her gown.

"You are truly gorgeous today, my wife," he said while kissing her shoulder as he unbuttoned her wedding dress, his hands easing up to feel her breasts. Doing so had been on his mind throughout the ceremony.

"You look mighty handsome, too, dear husband," she responded looking at him over her shoulder.

"Say that again," he whispered.

"You look mighty handsome, too, my dear husband," she softly repeated.

Gabe turned her fully towards him. Placing his hands at the back of her neck, he proceeded to show her his joy at hearing those words on her lips. Toni returned his passion. As usual, it did not take much before things turned hot. Toni started unbuttoning his shirt, smoothing her hands across his muscled chest. She bent her head to nip his chest with her teeth, causing him to sharply intake his breath.

"Baby, if you start that, we're definitely going to miss our flight," he said.

They parted ways before the embers turned to flames, and they had no care to stop them. They really did not want to miss their flight.

By mutual agreement, they had decided to wait on sex—strange, some would have thought, but they were sure about their love, and their wedding night would serve as the perfect physical expression of that love. They both knew what giving themselves to the wrong person meant, and neither wanted to jump the gun again. They were grown and knew it, but they were also committed to having a special night.

Shortly after changing clothes, they went to catch the charter flight for their honeymoon. Toni wanted to be cossetted in a log cabin—with snow—for their marriage trip, so that is what Gabe gave her. They landed in Montana, where a driver was waiting for them. A car was already at the rented cabin for their use. He hadn't wanted to drive to the house, but just sit with her while enjoying being a newly married couple.

After making it to the house, the driver removed their bags and placed them inside. Gabe picked up Toni and carried her across the threshold just as he did at their home in California.

"Again?" Toni laughingly asked.

"Absolutely."

"I love you," she told him, lightly kissing his chin.

"I love you, too."

They checked out the cabin while holding hands, but there was truly only one thing on each of their minds. A decision to wait to consummate their love meant months of cold showers for both of them, but they wanted to wait because they were sure. Without a doubt the passion burned strong and hot between them, but they wanted this night—their wedding night—to be like none other.

"Come here," he told her.

He put his hands on her face, leaned down, and kissed her with all the months of pent-up, unreleased passion. He was going to be her lover tonight. Not just of the heart, but of her body, as well.

Fiddlesticks! I hope I don't melt. Funnily, she recalled that long ago salon conversation. *I guess he's hot enough to melt chocolate.* She smiled.

"What's so funny?" he asked.

"I'll tell you later."

"Hmm."

He walked her up the stairs to the loft bedroom. He led her to sit on the bed, while he turned on his playlist from his phone, after connecting it to the Bluetooth speaker system in the room that he had requested of the owner's property manager. He had preset some wedding night music, and he knew just how to set the mood.

He started undoing the buttons on her blouse while they kissed. He eased her onto her back, opened the snap on her jeans, and started pulling them down while she raised her hips to help him with the task.

"You are so beautiful, Toni," he said while looking at her with that carnal heat in his eyes.

He unsnapped the front closure of her bra, taking in her beautiful brown mounds unfettered for the first time before him. *Good God. Thank You,* he thought. He traced the dark circle housing one of her nipples that was standing at attention. Toni gasped.

"Feels good, huh?"

"Yes, but you have on too many clothes."

"I can take care of that."

He undressed while Toni's eyes were on him the entire time. He dropped his boxers, and Toni's eyes widened a bit. Although she had felt him on previous occasions, the reality of what she thought he had was rather startling. *Well, well!* she smiled to herself with the thought.

"Okay?"

"Oh, yeah. Everything is just fine, baby," she whispered while her body increased its moisture, causing her to shift her hips. She lifted one of her hands from the bed to squeeze her breasts in an effort to ease some of the sudden pressure. The movement caused Gabe's eyes to darken to almost black.

Gabe rested on the bed with her, tossing the rest of her clothes on the floor, completely unconcerned about where they landed. His attention was one place and on one person only.

His long finger stroked her collarbone, moving down her shoulder to trace a sensuous path down her arm. The surveying of the landscape of her body continued with a trek on the underside of her arm and over to her luscious breasts. Teasingly, the finger tapped the tip of her other breast, but did not linger, making her gasp again. Her nipple cried out for attention, but its hunger would not be appeased at that moment.

The finger continued its trip down the right side of her body, tracing the indenture of her waist, the fullness of the hips the finger's owner loved, the long legs that held him captivated, only to increase Toni's frustration by tracing up the inside of her leg, her thigh, and alighting upon her core. He thumbed that nub of sensation that only had a single organic purpose—her pleasure.

"Gabe!" Toni's breath hitched. "What are you doing to me?"

"What your husband has a right to do. Loving you the best way I know how."

"Don't stop, baby," she begged squirming on the bed, "Please don't stop."

"No worries, Mrs. Jackson," he responded in a voice thick with passion, as he continued with his journey across her sexy body. "I'm not stopping anytime soon. We will do this *all* night."

"Mmm—," she moaned while rubbing her hands across his strong shoulders, feeling the muscles that accounted for his sexy strength, and remembering the dream from so many months ago.

They continued their exploration until neither of them could take anymore. Gabe lifted himself, and Toni raised her legs to allow him clear entry, gently placing her hands on his member to help guide him. Slowly, he eased himself into her tight walls, joining them in the timeless symbol of passionate love and two lives becoming one. Once all the way in, Gabe sighed in the way that one feels when walking into one's own home after a long trip and the thought of taking a rest in one's own bed. He was *home*. Toni joined his sigh with one of her own.

"I love you, Gabe."

"I love you, Toni."

They began the rock that singers have sung about for centuries. From Solomon with all his wives to contemporary artists, the dance between lovers has been worthy of putting pen to paper. They reveled in the connection that had been so hot between them from almost the beginning. Gabe's music selection highlighted their passion in a very sensual way.

Gabe raised one of Toni's legs to place it in the crook of his arm. The position allowed him to connect them more fully. Toni whispered all the love talk expected of a woman who was with her husband in *that* way. Unashamedly, she told him how good he was, how he needed to move, and how it all felt to her. He reciprocated, building the foundation for a fulfilling married sex life.

Neither had anticipated that their loving would be so good—that *speechless* kind of good—the first time. Toni's climax, followed by Gabe's, left them both without words, hearts beating, and wondering how quickly they could enjoy each other again.

Their lovemaking continued long into the night. Gabe and Toni were uninhibited in the expression of their love for one another. They touched each other. They tasted each other. They left no terrain unmarked. This was a lovers' loving—a lovers' fest—one in which they knew that there was much more to be celebrated than physical passion alone. This was lovemaking in its purest form. The kind between two people who knew that they had placed the deep part of themselves into the hands of someone who would care for and cherish it. This is what each had waited for, and it was worth the wait.

Toni flopped on Gabe's chest after a rather vigorous round of lovemaking.

"That. Was. Fan. Ta. Stic," she exhaled while trying to catch her breath. Sweat was dripping everywhere, and her body was still experiencing those small, delightful tremors that came from some good loving.

"So, you say, Woman. You're going to wear me out," his breath sounding choppy from his recent exertion. *This woman, this woman.*

Her enthusiasm in bed was more than he could have dreamed. He was indeed enjoying married life. Even with their busy schedules and the adjustment of living with another person—as neither had done so prior to being married, save for college roommates—his new bride had plenty of energy for the marriage bed—or, where they managed—that kept a genuine smile on his face.

He possessed a general air of satisfaction which did not go unnoticed by his longtime friend. Sam gave him a lot of payback in return for the jokes Gabe made during the first few months of his married life with Denni. They both agreed that there was sex, and then there was married sex. The concurrence was that married sex—with the right woman—was so much better.

"You'll be happily worn out," Toni teased with a very satisfied smile on her face, kissing his shoulder.

"Absolutely, sweetheart. Give me a few minutes, and I'll show you just how happy. You know, as well, that I am certified in melting chocolate, so keep right on talking trash," he teased in return, patting her on the butt while his heart beat out the drum known only to a well-loved man.

She had finally told him the salon story about a white man having to be "hot enough to melt chocolate".

"Baby, you ain't said but a —" Toni started but was interrupted by the ringing of her telephone.

"Who is that? It's 1AM," Gabe asked. "Gotta be Reecie or Alex."

Toni rolled over, stretching a bit since she loathed disconnecting their bodies, and pulled her phone from the nightstand.

"It's Reecie."

She tapped the green button.

"Reecie? Hi, Sis. Is everything okay?"

"Toni," she whispered.

"What? Why are you whispering?" Toni said, still breathing heavily.

"Why are you breathing so heavy?"

"Why do you think I'm breathing so heavily? It's the middle of the night, and I'm a newlywed. Now, what's wrong?"

"Sorry. Tell my brother-in-love "hi" for me," but she continued to whisper, "I'm in Vegas. I think I got married earlier today."

"What?!" Toni yelped, lifting up a bit more from Gabe's chest, to sit straight up.

"I think I got married earlier today," Reecie repeated in hushed tones.

"To whom?" Toni inquired.

"Justin Shaw."

"Who's he?"

"Opposing counsel."

"What?!" Toni exclaimed again.

"He's walking this way. I'll call you back." She quickly disconnected the call.

Toni dropped the phone on the bed, looking at Gabe in shock.

"What, baby?" Gabe asked, rubbing her back to calm her down.

"That was Reecie."

"Uh huh. Everything okay?"

"No. She said that she thinks she got married earlier today in Vegas. And, to top it off, to her opposing counsel!"

Catch Sherise "Reecie" Quinn's story in *To Tame a Lawyer*

www.ingramcontent.com/pod-product-compliance
Lightning Source LLC
Chambersburg PA
CBHW071824190726
48292CB00005B/1596